He smiled—agai̇[...]*ngs up for you?"*

She extended the handle on the suitcase and loaded her carry-on and laptop on top of it. "Thank you, but I have it."

Charlie leaned against the shuttle van and folded his arms across his chest. "I'll pick you up here a week from Sunday around three o'clock. I believe your plane leaves at six thirty."

"Yes, that would be wonderful. Do you have a number I can call, in case there's a problem?"

He stepped into the shuttle stairwell and thrust his hand into the glove box. Turning, he offered her a glossy orange business card balanced between his fingers. "Call this number and leave a message, ma'am. It's been my pleasure."

"Thank you, Mr. Parish. I'll see you Sunday then." Emily stuffed the card into the side pocket of her laptop. For a woman who had trained herself to control unwanted emotion, Emily felt totally spent from her brief encounter with Charlie Parish.

Anxious to put the unique and timely circumstances of the day behind her, she rushed with her luggage through puddles of water on the drive. The salty breeze teased her hair, and light fragrant drops of rain caught on her face until she got under the shelter of the overhanging roof. She stood there for a moment as her last hour with Charlie Parish competed with Stan's memory.

Blessed was the woman who had Charlie Parish's heart and chivalry. *Where did* that *thought come from?* No matter how nice the man came across, no matter how debonair or courteous he seemed, Charlie Parish's charisma would find its place in file thirteen and never resurface again.

DONNA L.
and writin
authors co
romance
American
and The
Her succes
led to her
Mayflower so
husband live in
beautiful blended family of six m
grandchildren, and three great-
find out more about her at www-

Don't miss out on any of our super romances.
address for information on our newest releases

Heartsong Presents Readers' Service
PO Box 721
Uhrichsville, OH 44683

Or visit www.heartsongpresents.com

Tropical Island Vows

Donna L. Rich

Heartsong Presents

Praise to the Lord for planting the dream in my heart to write. I dedicate this book to my husband, Nelson, who encouraged me to persevere to fulfill my dream and to my agent, Les, and my talented editors, JoAnne, Rachel, and Donna, for bringing my dream to life.

A note from the Author:
I love to hear from my readers! You may correspond with me by writing:

Donna L. Rich
Author Relations
PO Box 721
Uhrichsville, OH 44683

ISBN 978-1-61626-530-4

TROPICAL ISLAND VOWS

Copyright © 2011 by Donna L. Rich. All rights reserved. Except for use in any review, the reproduction or utilization of this work in whole or in part in any form by any electronic, mechanical, or other means, now known or hereafter invented, is forbidden without the permission of Heartsong Presents, an imprint of Barbour Publishing, Inc., PO Box 721, Uhrichsville, Ohio 44683.

Scripture taken from the Holy Bible, New International Version®. niv®. Copyright © 1973, 1978, 1984, 2010 by Biblica, Inc.™ Used by permission. All rights reserved.

This book is a work of fiction. Names, characters, places, and incidents are either products of the author's imagination or used fictitiously.

Our mission is to publish and distribute inspirational products offering exceptional value and biblical encouragement to the masses.

PRINTED IN THE U.S.A.

one

"Your conference call is ready, Mrs. Cameron."

Emily wrinkled her brows. She couldn't help but notice her dry uneven fingernail as she pressed the button on her telephone. Growing older certainly didn't come with any guarantees, but why did it take away her beautiful nails? "Hi girls! Got your tickets?"

"Hey yourself," Hattie gushed through her mellow South Carolina drawl. "I'm in Nashville on a design project. I'll fly out of here tomorrow at six o'clock in the evening."

"Straight to Florida?" Emily dusted the fine grit of her nail file across the tip of her thumbnail.

"No," said Linda. "She flies from Nashville to Dallas first."

"Ooh, I hate that airport." Emily took off her glasses and poked one temple arm between her teeth. "When are you leaving, Linda?"

"I'm scheduled to fly out of Indy at 6:55 tomorrow morning. By the way, I dug out a few pictures of the three of us back when we all attended Butler. I'll bring them along so we can reminisce."

"Linda, I have one question," said Emily. "Do we want to see how young we looked way back when?"

Hattie chimed in. "Come on, girls. I haven't changed that much!"

"Ha! I actually believe you're right about that, Hattie. Anyway, too bad we couldn't have met in Indy and all taken the same flight down to Tampa. Linda, are you going to fly straight to Tampa?" Emily pinched a piece of lint from her pants then dropped it into the wastebasket at the side of her desk. She smiled to herself. If Linda had to opt for a flight with three layovers and a ride on the engine, she'd do it to save money.

"No, I have one stop in Atlanta first. I hope I make my connection smoothly. There's not more than an hour between flights."

"Well, I owe a debt of gratitude to you girls for insisting the three of us drop everything and go on vacation before my busy season starts at the office." Linda and Hattie had included Emily in their yearly trip south. With Emily still emotionally connected to her husband Stan, who died a year earlier, her friends wanted to help her cut the ties. In Emily's mind, they wanted her to find someone else.

"Pray for me, Emily," said Hattie. "I'm beginning to get worked up over traveling into Dallas. I remember what you said about your last flight there. Didn't someone at the ticket counter give away your seat because you were delayed on the tarmac for a half hour? If I get hung up in that airport, I know I'll just die."

"Pray for all of us, Em," said Linda. "It's about time one of us widows links up with that special man."

Emily smiled to herself. At least her friends realized she prayed. "I don't think I could be as close to anyone as I was to Stan. Anyway, what could happen in ten days?"

"Maybe you'll be able to move on once you scatter Stan's ashes. Are you still going to?" asked Linda.

"I am if I can get through security with him. I'm thinking of emptying his ashes into a small box."

"Emily, you're crazy. Just take the urn," said Hattie. "I think you're allowed to do that."

"We'll see. I'll have to do some investigating. Anyway, I've made the decision to sprinkle his ashes in the Gulf, just the way he wanted. I checked into it, and you can do that if the boat takes you out to a legal distance."

"It'll all work out," said Linda.

Emily glanced at the clock. "Hey girls, I have heaps of papers to go through before I head over to my hair stylist. She's going to cover my gray roots and weave some blond through the haystack, so I look younger than. . . Well, never mind how young. See you on the island."

"Love ya, Em," said Hattie.

"Yeah, love both of you," said Linda.

"You know I love you both. Have fun, and be careful." Emily clicked off. She brushed a few loose gray hairs from her shoulders, slipped the red silk-blend jacket from her slender arms, and eased it over the back of her chair.

Emily loved the feel of that suit. It fit well. Even so, she had decided to leave luxury behind for ten days. Her eyes drifted across the room to the box with her online Walmart order that sat on the shelf under her printer table.

Using her toes, she nudged the back of each pump off her heels, taking a moment to scrunch her feet into the office's plush carpet, a luxury afforded to Stan when he was president of the consulting company. She sighed. They would have been married forty-five years on Friday.

Emily's youngest son, Jason, fully understood Emily's need to move past Stan's death. At Christmas, he'd jokingly mentioned it was about time she began dating. Jennifer's scrunched brows and Jared's swift elbow into Jason's side made it clear her oldest two didn't feel the same.

Her eyes fell on a stack of papers that needed to be dealt with before she left. Hopefully, this trip would be a launching point for her. Emily was about to do something to start her own business after forty-five faithful years of working with Stan's. Pulling in a Florida account would be a giant step toward growing her company apart from Cameron Consultants and away from Indiana.

The lure of the tropics had inspired her to draw up a proposal for the Florida citrus company run by Roger Parish. She had tried for months to get him to commit to a meeting. Fortunately, he had responded and called her twice at her home in the last week to set something up. The timing couldn't be better. She lifted the proposal from her pile of papers, situated it in a file folder, and stuck it in her briefcase.

Her receptionist buzzed in on the intercom. "Mrs. Cameron?"

"Yes, Anna."

"Sorry to interrupt. Jackson Underwood is on line one. He wants to know about dinner tonight."

Jackson had been one of the men to whom Stan had once considered selling the business. Emily knew that Jackson wanted to talk about purchasing the company. "I already told him I wasn't available. Inform him I'm out of commission until next week sometime, and I'll call him then."

"I told him that. Problem is, he's on his way up the elevator now."

Emily clicked off the intercom and slipped her feet back into her shoes. Why couldn't the man understand the word no? She thrust her arms into her jacket sleeves, pulled it on over her white shell, and buttoned the middle button.

The intercom buzzed again. Anna's voice came across apologetically. "Mrs. Cameron? Mr. Underwood is here."

Emily squeezed the nose pads on her new Burberry framed glasses closer together before she pushed the temple arms past her high cheekbones. *Okay, what's got you so angry, Emily? Your reluctance to meet with Jackson or your anger that he has selective hearing?* "Please, send him in, Anna." She walked across to the door, breathed deeply as she pasted on her business look, and reached for the doorknob just as Jackson pushed into the room.

"You're a hard lady to get hold of, Emily." His lips formed a grim line.

"Sorry, Jackson." She issued a bogus smile. "I'm just not going to be able to connect with you tonight. I'm leaving tomorrow for Florida and I want to have every document cleaned off my desk before I go."

Emily turned to walk to her desk, and he followed close on her heels.

"Are you sure you don't want to reconsider and have dinner? I really want to discuss the plans my attorneys have drawn up regarding purchasing the company from you."

"Can't right now, Jackson. Everyone who wants a piece of this company is in the same boat. I'll inform all of you of my decision, when I return." Emily moved behind her desk. "You will excuse me now, won't you? I have at least six hours of paperwork to muddle through."

"Forgive my persistence, but doesn't the board make a collective decision on ownership?"

Emily looked up from her papers. "Actually, Stan has put me in complete control of that decision."

"Oh. Very well. Can you at least call me when you get there, Emily? Perhaps I can get a flight and meet you. I'm serious about getting something from you in writing as soon as possible."

Emily cringed. The bottom line for Jackson was money and notoriety. Stan built the company by being customer-friendly and cost efficient. Because of that, she had considered selling to Stan's brother, Carson, whom Stan had trained to follow in his footsteps. "Jackson, I'm committed to Stan's values when it comes to this company." Emily shuffled some papers and lifted one eyebrow toward him. "Now, if you wouldn't mind..."

"Very well, Emily. I'll call you in ten days. Have a restful trip." He edged out the door then briefly stuck his head back in. "Please don't shut me out of this deal."

Emily knew she'd never consider Jackson's deal. Meanwhile, this initial refusal had gone better than she'd thought. As the door clicked shut, Emily opened her top desk drawer and pulled out the elegant, basket-weave silver frame that held her fortieth wedding anniversary photo. She stared at the attractive man who would have sacrificed his life before his moral principles and business standards.

Oh, Stan, I still can't believe you're gone. Everything seems so surreal. Now I need to honor your wishes by doing this ashes thing. Emily frowned. She and Stan had an understanding that went back to when they first walked the beach as newlyweds. He'd wanted his ashes sprinkled out over the warm Gulf waters when he died. Emily had been strongly opposed to his wishes, but each time they visited the Gulf he'd made his desire clear to her. He wouldn't budge on the matter.

He still had more pepper than salt in his hair in the photo, and the twinkle in his eye sparkled right out of the frame. His arm rested on her shoulder, and her head lay on his. *I'm not sure I can do this, Stan, but it's what you wanted me to do.* A tear surfaced at her lid, but she quickly dabbed it away. Staring at his face only exacerbated her still simmering frustration at her husband for leaving her so soon. She put the picture back, felt side down next to one of her pocket-size Bibles, and closed the drawer.

Emily's friends in the business world told her Stan's brother would be the best choice to run the firm, if she didn't want to take it on permanently. Nevertheless, Emily knew she had the no-nonsense, get-down-to-business talent to grow the company. The ticket to becoming Indianapolis' most successful woman remained hers for the taking. But she still wasn't sure what she wanted.

Her appointment with Roger Parish would be the first test to see if she could start her own company down south. She could run it at her own pace and not according to the dictates of the board of directors for Cameron Consultants.

I wish I could break through this stalemate in my own mind. Do I want the business, or not? Maybe I should pray. Would God hear me? It would be nice to have Carson take over for a time. Then she could extend her vacation to more than ten days. She could forget about the business in Indianapolis and simply act as though she were another tourist hitting the beach in Florida.

She knew one thing. Except for her one business appointment in Bradenton, for at least ten days, she didn't want to be known as president of Cameron Consultants. For ten days she wanted to be Emily Nobody and meet new people who didn't know her identity. For ten days, she wanted to be accepted for herself and not for her name.

&

The shrill cries of willets and sandpipers populating the narrow strip of sandbar outside Charlie Parish's beach house alerted him to the breaking of a new day. He tugged at the silk-like sheet, damp from the overnight humidity, and pulled it up over his shoulders. The song of the surf lulled him back to sleep, but before long, he turned his half-opened eyes to the left where Nancy's sweet smile had once greeted him every morning. The painful memory of her death two years ago stabbed into his gut.

His body rolled to the right where the sliding door framed an unforgettable panorama of daylight moving in over the open waters of the Gulf. A school of dolphins somersaulted across the lapping waves, the marine mammals showing off their repertoire of water gymnastics.

The aroma of coffee, already dripping into the pot, jolted

him from the bed until he awakened enough to remember that he didn't have to get up early. His son, Roger, now held the position as president of Southland Citrus.

Charlie lifted his white terry cloth robe from the back of the chair near the open screen door. He thrust his arm into one sleeve, but then a whiff of mildew found his nose. He promptly lifted the lid on the wicker clothes hamper and threw in the robe. Even the high humidity wouldn't force him to give up his passion for sleeping at night with his windows open.

Nevertheless, he lived in Florida, and every morning he closed the windows, flicked the indicator on his thermostat to air conditioner, and set the temperature to seventy-four. He had no sooner done it today than a double thud landed on his front door.

"Mr. Parish? I'm here to clean. Can you let me in, please?" The perky, dark-eyed daughter of one of his former Hispanic employees had taken the job of cleaning Charlie's house every other week. Charlie had become close to the family back in the days when he donned sweatshirts and jeans and joined his workers in the groves to pick fruit. He'd be surprised if Roger ever did that.

He knew he should hire Tess to come every week to clean, but she was so orderly he could never find where she put anything after she left. He leaned into the kitchen, hoping his shout would be heard through the door. "Give me a minute, Tess. I'm still in my pajamas."

Two cedar-lined closets in Charlie's bedroom held differing wardrobes of clothing. Anxious to change the business image that had defined him for so many years, he opened the closet that held everyday sports clothes—attire that would help Charlie Parish shed the corporate stuffiness that had been so much a part of his persona.

He slid each hanger across the rod until he came to the GOD's GYM T-shirt. The freshness of spring-scented fabric softener smoothed across his nose as he tugged the shirt over his head.

When he yanked at his khaki trousers, the gold hanger spun around a few times before it left the rod and dropped to the floor on top of two others. His favorite green sports shirt, with well-spaced sailboats in the pattern, would go well with the khakis. After he tied a narrow flax-colored cord sporting a coquina shell around his neck, he covered his head with a straw Panama hat. A splash of Old Spice on his cheeks sealed his image for the day.

Two more thuds on the door. "I have another house to clean, Mr. Parish."

Charlie winced at the terse voice as he trekked across the kitchen floor into the foyer. "I'm sorry, Tess. I'm coming." He pushed against the massive door to loosen the dead bolt and swung it open. "Come in, honey. I didn't get up when I should have. You're such a good girl to come all the way over here to clean. Your mom drive you?"

Tess stepped ahead of Charlie into the kitchen. "No, my brother, Hector, rode me out here in his Jeep."

Charlie hurried to the counter and pulled a twenty-dollar bill from his wallet. He reached for her hand and tucked the money into her palm. "This is for having to wait for me to open the door."

Tess shrugged her shoulders as a blush grazed her face. "Mr. Parish, I haven't even cleaned yet. You don't have to pay me extra."

A smile puckered on her face when he reached to pat her on the shoulder. "The upstairs theater room won't have to be cleaned yet. Your check is right over there by the blender. Hungry?" Charlie picked two doughnuts out of a waxed bag sitting on the counter.

"No, thanks. You know me. Up early, bagel and juice, off to work. You shouldn't eat that doughnut, Mr. Parish. Not good for you." She tilted her head. "Mrs. Parish wouldn't have let you eat that stuff on a regular basis. You need to get another wife to help you stay healthy."

"You know Roger probably wouldn't like it one bit if I found a new wife." Charlie nodded to her with a careful smile.

Having taken the spray cleaner out from under the kitchen sink, Tess started to walk out of the room, stopped in the doorway, then turned to Charlie. "He just doesn't realize older people still fall in love. He'd understand. I know he wants you to be happy."

Older people? As Tess left the room, Charlie shrugged then glanced at the counter where the envelope containing the day's schedule lay. The decision to buy the shuttle and go into business with his brother, Les, had already proven to be fruitful. Les agreed to run the business side of the venture while Charlie agreed to do the actual pickups at the airport. Les's daughter would help Charlie out when she could, and Les promised to help in an emergency only.

Charlie rinsed out a mug he had used the day before, poured himself a cup of coffee, and then removed the day's schedule from the envelope. He situated his reading glasses in place and ran his finger down the list of flights. The American flight from Indianapolis and the Southwest flight from Pittsburgh would both arrive at Tampa International before four o'clock. A family of seven from Pennsylvania, named DeMarco, three college students from IU, and one woman, Emily Cameron, from Indianapolis, made up his passengers.

Charlie shoved the rest of the glazed doughnut into his mouth then washed it down with the last swallow of coffee. Linking his arm through the strap on his well-worn leather briefcase, he locked the door behind him. While he meandered down the wooden steps of the three-story beach house, he plucked a magnolia blossom from the tree that spread its shade over the yard. The blossom sucked tight against his nose as he sniffed its fragrance. *Am I ready for another wife?*

As he headed for the luxury conversion van in the driveway, he spared a glance under the beach house at the canvas-covered Buick Le Sabre that he had purchased years back for driving between the island and the mainland. The cost of operating it had been much cheaper than Nan y's old Mercedes that sat covered next to it. He still d ve the Mercedes on special occasions.

Once inside the van, he snatched a plastic spray bottle out of his small duffle. Even he caught the lingering tennis shoe aroma from the last group of athletes that rode cut to the island from the airport. The three puffs of orange-blossom scent came close to being the next best thing to being back in the groves, working.

Tess didn't have to tell him he ate the wrong things. His hand locked around an orange from inside the paper bag that held his lunch, and he considered that enough health for one day. He chuckled as he peeled the skin from the navel—a California navel. Roger would have a fit over the disloyalty.

Daring to flip the visor down, he examined his face as the next peel of orange zest misted on his hand. The mirror laid bare the truth. Nancy's death had stilled his desire to stay healthy or work out.

His hat set off a rotund appearance. Smile wrinkles surrounded his dimples, a little puffiness sat under the eyes, and jowls formed at the corners of his lips. He pulled the Ray-Bans from the glove box and positioned them on his face. Maybe Tess was right. He needed to eat healthier and work out more. *But it's no fun to be healthy alone.*

two

Emily slipped her arm through her purse straps, squeezed the laptop case handle, and hugged the carry-on against her body as her patent leather sling-back pumps clicked across the floor of the M80 jet. The urn, packed inside her carry-on, had passed through security without a problem.

She had barely passed from the jet bridge onto the concourse when her cell rang. Her daughter's number showed on the display. "Hi Jennifer, how are you?"

"Mom, I've changed my mind. I want to be there when you sprinkle Dad's ashes."

Emily marveled how Jennifer had grown to be devoted to Stan as if he were her natural father. Of course, she had never known any other. Nevertheless, Jennifer's words sounded curt and offhand. "Now, calm down honey. It's going to be okay."

"Mom, I know we decided you should do this on your own, but I'm afraid I'll always regret not being there. Can I come?"

The distress in Jennifer's voice melted Emily's heart. "Of course you may come. I won't do anything until you get here."

"Do you have the urn?"

"I have it with me."

"Is this hard for you to do?"

"This is the most difficult thing I've ever done. I'm glad you'll be with me."

"Mom, are you sure this is what you *want* to do?"

"Dad wanted this. For some reason, his Bohemian thinking kicked in back in the sixties, and he made the decision. Now, no matter what we want, it's up to us to follow through."

"Where are you going to be? I'm coming down. Please, don't do a thing until I get there."

"Jennifer, I promise."

"For some reason, I just need another chance to say good-bye."

"I feel the exact same way, honey. I don't know if we'll ever arrive at the place where we feel we've finalized our farewells, but I hope so."

"Me, too. I can get a connection out of Fort Wayne and be there by tomorrow."

"I'll wait. You remember where Dad and I used to go near Bradenton Beach?"

"That place you showed me out on Anna Maria?"

"That's where Hattie, Linda, and I will be. Call me when you land."

"Will do, Mom. I love you."

While the aroma of brewing coffee and fast-food chicken teased her empty stomach, Emily peeled the paper from an energy bar she'd stuck in her pocket earlier and bit off a small piece. She'd never been able to eat before she flew in an airplane. A tasty evening meal sounded good about now. However, she had a shuttle to meet.

The carry-on held her pink tennis shoes and two inexpensive summer outfits, which she had packed snugly around Stan's urn. She hadn't had time to try them on. Nevertheless, some kind of corporate grit kicked in and gave her the desire to put her well-to-do mind-set to rest for ten days.

Could she actually kill the mentality that had coerced her into buying only the most expensive clothes for the past ten years? In spite of the Walmart purchase, she hadn't gotten to that point yet. Her suitcase held equal amounts of both because she rationalized she had to have nice clothes along for her meeting with Roger Parish.

Emily glanced at her watch. Her instructions indicated the shuttle always left on time. Since she had a half hour before she had to be there, she ducked into the nearest restroom and changed out of her business attire and into some of her recent purchases. Then she headed for the baggage claim.

While she strode through the airport, thoughts rumbled around in her mind of how she hadn't spent very much time lately reading her Bible or praying. As soon as she decided to make up for it by praying right there and then, her cell rang.

"Emily?"

"Linda, you sound harried."

"I am harried. My worst fears were realized. I'm still in Atlanta. I missed my connection and they're trying to get me on another flight. No matter, though. I couldn't have flown any cheaper. I guess you'll be there for a while before I get there."

"I'm at Tampa now. I'll see you when you get to the inland. Take care." Emily clicked her phone shut as she continued to the baggage area. She'd had a feeling that Linda would have problems. Linda made good money and could have afforded a better flight. However, she saved and invested most of it to use when she retired. *You always get what you pay for.*

By the time Emily got to the lower level for the baggage claim, she found her large Gucci trolley had been knocked from the conveyor to the floor. With her handbag straps pushed onto her shoulder, she attached the carry-on and the laptop to the extended handle of her suitcase, and then tugged them a short distance to a car-rental counter. "Can you tell me where I'm supposed to catch the shuttle for Anna Maria Island? My secretary told me there'd be one waiting."

The woman behind the desk nudged her colleague and

motioned her head to Emily. "Did you read the sign? This is a car-rental service not a shuttle service. You need to make your way down to the ground transportation kiosk." Her slender finger with the long red acrylic nail pointed east.

Wanting to vent her displeasure to the woman, Emily thought better of it and walked toward the kiosk. *A soft answer turns away anger, Emily. Get to the man up ahead with kind eyes.*

The older gentleman's attention was locked on the scene across the aisle where three screaming children sat next to a teenager, presumably their sister. Emily moved in front of him. "Excuse me, can you tell me where I can get the shuttle for Anna Maria Island?"

He turned to her and said, "I sure can. All shuttles are supposed to wait in two different areas, ma'am—you can head to the right or left, then to the end of each hall and through the doors. If your shuttle is not there, head for the opposite door."

Emily's head throbbed. Having always been of the opinion the only dumb question was the one not asked, she wished this time she hadn't asked. At first, she headed for the east door, then somehow, through all the fog in her mind, she remembered Anna's directions had indicated the shuttle would be waiting for her at the west door.

The word *shuttle* conjured up images from her last ride at the Chicago airport where smelly bodies packed tightly into the car and little air-conditioning left her nauseated the rest of the day. With any luck, the shuttle would be gone and she could rent a taxi for the ride to Anna Maria Island. *Come on, Emily. Try to be a normal person and ride the shuttle.*

As she trudged toward the door, she spied a luxury conversion van, full of people, sitting curbside with the name NANCY BELLE decaled on the front door. A man about her age, not much taller than her five feet two inches with average dress and sporting a Panama hat, walked toward her after she exited the building.

"Ma'am, are you Mrs. Cameron?" Sophisticated and charming, the gentleman took off his hat, smiled, and reached out his hand.

She engaged her swift firm handshake but was surprised at his gentle grip. After a brief hello, she pulled her hand away. "How did you know who I was?"

"My family of seven from Pennsylvania is already seated, and so are my IU students. You are my last passenger of the day unless Mr. Cameron is traveling with you also."

"Oh no, there's no Mr. Cameron. I'm widowed."

"Oh, I'm sorry, ma'am."

"That's quite all right."

He looked at her baggage. "Is this all your luggage?"

Emily revolved her wedding band around her finger as she scanned the length of the van that looked more like an RV. The inside had luxurious leather covering the driver's captain chair in the front and all the other seats behind his. *This might be more comfortable than I thought.* "If there's not enough room, I can take a taxi."

"I can call you a taxi, but you'll have a much more comfortable ride with me. If you'll just bear with me, I'll get things settled in there and make room for you on the first seat on the right side. Don't you worry. Are you okay? Here, let me take your Gucci and your carry-on."

His voice could lull a baby to sleep. A smile broke open on his face, revealing perfectly aligned, white teeth as he nodded toward the van. "You never know who's going to show up on those planes. One day I had a family with nine kids. Stair steps, they were. My hour-and-a-half trip out to the beach seemed like ten hours. I had to stop twice to allow some of the kids to use the restroom. This trip won't be near as bad, trust me."

Emily brightened at his steady, but warm, eye contact. Pleasantly tactful and well mannered, his careful explanation of the circumstances with his van immediately settled her doubt. One side of her mouth curled on her freckled face then relented a little more. She gripped the handle of her carry-on as her other hand held tightly to her laptop and handbag. "Thank you, Mr. . . ."

"Parish. Charlie Parish."

His smile provoked one from her. "Thank you, Mr. Charlie Parish."

"Here, you wait right here outside the door, and I'll stow your luggage in the overhead compartment. Welcome to Florida. I can't imagine why anyone would ever want to live in Indiana."

Although she wanted to breathe in the warm Florida air, all she could smell was exhaust from the shuttle and surrounding airplanes. She shaded her eyes and watched the suntanned man prod the young boy in the front seat to move back with his parents. He swiped his left hand across the seat, then crouched and offered her his right hand.

As she wondered what he brushed off the seat, her question was answered when a child's voice from the back of the shuttle screamed, "Mommy, where's my M&M's?"

Emily took Charlie's hand as he ushered her up the two steps into the shuttle. She looked down at her carry-on, knowing the urn was inside, then let her eyes stray to the man whose gallant action reminded her of Stan's chivalry when he was alive. *It's only a woman's natural response to the human touch, Emily. Nothing more.* "Thank you." Any further words lodged in her throat as his courteous behavior held her attention.

Charlie stood next to his seat while his eyes scanned each passenger. "Everyone buckled up? We're ready to roll to the beach." He turned an eye on Emily and lowered his voice to a whisper. "Fasten your belt, ma'am. These freeways around here are dangerous. You might say it feels like the Daytona 500 once you get out on Interstate 75."

Emily set her purse on the floor and nodded as the power of suggestion from Hattie and Linda about wanting her to meet a man in Florida flustered her. He had a sense of humor. Her hand tightened around the laptop case, and her feet crunched into multicolored, candy-coated chocolate, as her apprehension festered just under the surface.

"I'm sorry to hover, ma'am, but it's the law. Need help with that belt?"

Shaken out of her reflections, Emily then realized Mr. Parish had taken a firm stand in front of her as his hand grasped the upper part of her seat belt. She swiveled her head behind her to see the impatient passengers who had glued their eyes to her and Charlie.

An unwelcome reflex thrust her hand to grab the belt out of his. "I have it, thank you." She valiantly fought to keep the heat from emerging on her face at her annoyance with herself. Nevertheless, she felt it manifest itself in full array. Tugging to pull the belt from the side, she snapped it in place then offered him a quick nod of acknowledgment.

A grin nearly swallowed his face as he turned to slide in behind the steering wheel. Was he laughing at her?

Emily's teeth clenched automatically as she turned her head toward the disappearing airport, pulled a magazine from a side pocket in her laptop case, and began fanning herself. When was the last time she'd helplessly lost her composure over a man's good manners? In fact, when had Emily Cameron *ever* lost her composure?

❧

The children's clamoring and bickering back and forth reminded Emily of her grandchildren's sibling rivalry. However, the noise soon lowered to a drone as the shuttle's motion rocked the younger children to sleep.

The hum of the wheels lulled Emily into a daydreaming zone of her own as they trekked out to the narrow strip of land with the Gulf of Mexico traveling down the west side and the bay traveling down the east. She found herself already wishing she had more time to spend on Anna Maria Island.

The shuttle eventually veered off the interstate at the Bradenton exit past Cracker Barrel, a smattering of restaurants, motels, and gas stations, then followed the heavily traveled Manatee Avenue to the beach. A couple miles down the road, Charlie looked into his rearview mirror. "Please take note of Manatee Memorial Hospital on your right. You never know when you might need one. As we head through the main downtown area, you'll probably notice the dearth of high rises in our city. You'll note that the island is the same. There are no tall hotels or condominiums to close you in."

Just then, Charlie accidentally veered into half of another lane. The woman he cut off laid on her horn. Charlie shrugged his shoulders in an apology as the IU students chuckled. "Let me also point out the raging rush hour drivers. Most of them are people my age."

Charlie had a smile that was hard to resist, but any time Emily noticed herself staring at his reflection in his rearview mirror, she abruptly shifted her gaze to look out the window on her right.

The sun dwindled, and a moan escaped her lips as threatening clouds rolled between her and the sun. The vehicle crossed over the drawbridge on Manatee Avenue, heading west just as a thunderstorm moved in the opposite direction.

Loud thunderclaps awakened the children. The syncopated raindrops on the windshield sounded more like hail and served as an unwelcome background for the children who were now complaining they wouldn't get to go swimming.

"It won't last long. Give it an hour or two. By the time you're unpacked, it'll be past." Charlie nodded to them from his mirror. Then he looked at Emily. This time she didn't look away quickly enough and smiled back.

Emily's fingers tapped on her laptop case as she looked behind her to the other passengers. Her eyes flitted one more time to the mirror in front of her when the van made a left turn onto Bay Drive.

In a few blocks, Charlie pulled into a parking lot at a group of condos on Gulf Drive North where he dropped off the family of seven. After Charlie helped to unload their luggage, he drove two blocks down a back street to drop the IU students at a bungalow in a residential neighborhood. Before he drove away, he turned around to Emily. "Looks like you're down on the beach front, is that correct?"

"Yes, I'm down toward Bradenton Beach." She had rented the same condominium that she and Stan had rented for so many years in a row. At one point, they had talked about buying it. The cost was too prohibitive then. If only they had known how the value would climb in the following years.

She hugged her carry-on against her chest. "The complex comes up quickly. Before you know it, you could pass it by."

"I know this area fairly well, but I think I have the incorrect address. Do you know the name of it?"

"I hate to tell you this but. . .we just passed it."

"No problem. I'll just head down a few blocks and turn around. This traffic behind me stretches back about two blocks. Trust me, if I'd stop now, I'd have a honking, angry mess." He made a sudden left turn onto a side street, turned around, and headed back north on Gulf Drive.

"There, it's that cement-looking one, two buildings up."

Charlie waited for traffic to pass, then turned in. "Here you are, ma'am." He turned off the motor and clicked the button on his seat belt. "I know this is the right place."

"Thank you, so much, for everything today." She unlocked her seat belt, stood, and opened the compartment above her to reach her suitcase. Just as quickly, she felt a touch as soft as Charlie's voice on her shoulder.

"Excuse me. That's my job, ma'am. Here, let me take it out for you." Charlie lifted her suitcase and took it outside the door to the pavement.

Emily clutched her laptop case against her chest, laced the carry-on across her other shoulder, then placed her hand in the one offered by Charlie as she made her way down the van steps and onto the sidewalk.

He smiled—again. "May I carry these things up for you?"

She extended the handle on the suitcase and loaded her carry-on and laptop on top of it. "Thank you, but I have it."

Charlie leaned against the shuttle and folded his arms across his chest. "I'll pick you up here a week from Sunday around three o'clock. I believe your plane leaves at six-thirty."

"Yes, that would be wonderful. Do you have a number I can call, in case there's a problem?"

He stepped into the shuttle stairwell and thrust his hand into the glove box. Turning, he offered her a glossy orange business card balanced between his fingers. "Call this number and leave a message, ma'am. It's been my pleasure."

"Thank you, Mr. Parish. I'll see you Sunday then." Emily stuffed the card into the side pocket of her laptop. For a woman who had trained herself to control unwanted emotion, Emily felt totally spent from her brief encounter with Charlie Parish.

Anxious to put the unique and timely circumstances of the day behind her, she rushed with her luggage through puddles of water on the drive. The salty breeze teased her hair, and light fragrant drops of rain caught on her face until she got under the shelter of the overhanging roof. She stood there for a moment as her last hour with Charlie Parish competed with Stan's memory.

Blessed was the woman who had Charlie Parish's heart and chivalry. *Where did* that *thought come from?* No matter how nice the man came across, no matter how debonair or courteous he seemed, Charlie Parish's charisma would find its place in file thirteen and never resurface again.

three

Emily lugged everything up the stairs at once. She eased her bags to the floor of the landing, took the large envelope from RFY Vacations out of her briefcase, and ripped the end of the envelope off with her teeth to retrieve her rental instructions. The code for the lock had changed since the last time she'd been here. After she entered the numbers on the key box, chimes playing "My Dog Has Fleas" signaled a correct entry, allowing her to open the box and retrieve her key.

She held the door open with her foot as she wheeled the suitcase inside. The top-heavy Gucci fell to its side as her laptop and carry-on dropped beside it. She scurried to pick up her carry-on and opened it to retrieve the urn, checking to make sure the lid had remained secure. She dropped the set of apartment keys on the glass dining room table with a clink then meandered toward the sliding door that faced the Gulf.

A balm of warm breezes salted with the scent of rain rushed in through the open door as she stepped out onto the screened lanai. How could anyone doubt God's existence with the panorama that stretched out before her? She stood there for a few minutes, letting the current of air relax her frazzled nerves. The rain had slowed. She folded her arms in satisfaction that she had at least accomplished getting safely to her destination in spite of the adventure and confusion churning in her belly.

Water ran in rivulets off the plastic chair cushions as she turned them onto the cement floor of the lanai. She rushed into the kitchen to get a towel and returned to wipe the remaining residue off. She swiped once across the glass table then set the urn with Stan's ashes on top of it. *For the first time since you died, Stan, I think I can do this. I've walked by your remains each day as they sat in the urn on the hutch. I've thought about you constantly, but now I have to let go for my own peace of mind. You're not really here anymore, and I have to come to grips with that.*

Eventually, the rain stopped and the clouds dissipated, allowing the sun to begin its impressive display. Awed at the sense nothing more beautiful existed, she stared at the fiery blob that hung three inches above the horizon. A perfect moment had come for her to separate from Stan.

Within seconds, she found herself running toward the coast, clutching the urn in both hands. Her steps slowed as the edge of the waves bore three gulls to the shore where others scavenged. They flocked around her when she stooped to the fringe of the waves. After shooing the birds off, Emily couldn't bring herself to do it. She couldn't empty the ashes.

The gulls landed in sequence on the waves while the sun spilled like molten lava into the water. She had been careless in thinking the perfect moment had arrived. She had gotten carried away with the sunset and the surf and hadn't stopped to think about Jennifer.

A flood of assurance came to her from the God she had always known. That voice that so often comforted her in the past still whispered to her now. *"I have you in the palm of My hand, Emily. Don't be afraid to let go of your past and trust Me for the unconditional love you need."*

As soon as the words passed through her mind, peace rushed into her heart. Even so, she quickly reverted to another mode. Was it really okay to move on and accept the future God had prepared for her?

❧

Charlie flicked on the accessory light above the driver's seat and read down through the list of passenger names until he came to Mrs. Cameron's. He pressed the dialer icon on the touch pad of his phone then keyed in her number.

Emily answered on the fourth ring.

"Mrs. Cameron? This is Charlie, the shuttle driver. I was cleaning out the van after my deliveries, and I wondered if you had missed your purse yet. It was sitting on the floor under your seat. May I bring it back?"

"I'm at the beach right now. Can you give me an approximate time you'll be here?"

"Maybe about ten to fifteen minutes, depending on traffic."

"That would be great. I'll meet you at the bottom of my stairs."

Charlie drove back and parked in the rental's drive. He clutched the soft straw bag against his chest as he held in the bulging contents with his other hand. Emily was obviously a woman of simple means, yet she had fashionable tastes that set her apart from other women. While he smelled the lingering scent on her handbag, he wondered how any woman could stuff so much junk into one small bag. He pressed his nose against it, breathing in the flowery fragrance that he remembered from picking her up earlier in the day.

She wasn't at the stairway yet, so he waited for her in the midst of clusters of red and pink azaleas, which hung from wrought-iron staffs in the side yard of the condo. As the glow of twilight fused through the air, he saw Mrs. Cameron as she began her trek back up toward the rental.

"Classy woman," he muttered. Charlie gave in to the realization that he wanted to find out more about her. As he stepped out of the flora and into the light that shone from the nearby lamppost, Emily paused at the sea oats. "Is that you, Mr. Parish?"

Charlie touched the brim of his Panama hat and gave a nod of his head to acknowledge her. "I hope I didn't startle you."

She walked closer and pointed to the bulge in his arms. "I just wanted to make sure it was you. I didn't even realize I left that in the van." She took the bag from him and scooped the leather straps up over her shoulder. "I would have noticed after it was too late to call you. Thank you. I owe you for that."

Charlie diverted his gaze from the urn in her hand and motioned to the complex. "This is a beautiful group of condominiums."

Emily walked to the first step then turned. "It's nice to have two friends sharing the unit with me and sharing expenses."

Charlie walked a few steps in the direction of his shuttle, unable to keep a smile from coming across his face. Whatever her reasons were for staying here, she had settled about fifteen minutes from his beach house. "You have my card should you have any questions while you're out here on the beach."

As she walked up a few more steps, her face seemed to concentrate on him. "Maybe I'll see you again, then?"

He tipped his hat in leaving. "Maybe you will."

❧

Since there were no fast food restaurants on the island, Charlie drove back over to the mainland to go to Boston Market. On his way, he stopped at the car wash on Cortez Road to get the van ready for the next run. He swept the inside then quickly sprayed down the outside to get rid of the dust. As he stepped back into the shuttle, the Pink Panther theme Roger's wife, Joyce, had programmed into his cell phone, started playing.

"Hello, Rog."

"Dad, it's not Roger; it's me, Joyce. Are you coming for dinner?"

"Oh honey, I'm sorry. I got sidetracked."

"You have time, Dad. Rog has just arrived home and is in the shower. He thought we all might be able to talk about those retirement villas on the water. Are you in town or out at the beach?"

He sighed. Roger and Joyce meant well. They had been trying for months to convince him to sell his beach house and move into a retirement village where he wouldn't have any maintenance or upkeep. Then he could rent out the beach house to pay for the villa. Now that he had turned the company over to Roger, Charlie had plenty of time to putter around the house, and he didn't need the extra money. "I'm on my way back to the beach, hon. Forgive me, and I'll make it up to you guys."

"No need, Dad. We're just worried about you being out there on the beach. Don't you get lonely? We wish you could be closer so you can be more involved in Buddy and Belle's activities. Before long, they'll think they're too old to spend time with any of us."

Charlie loved it that his kids were concerned for his welfare, but the grandkids loved coming to the beach. How could he throw that away and move to a sterile compact condo? "I'll try to get to more of their sporting events. Can you e-mail me a schedule so I know when they are? We're not that far from each other."

"I will, Dad."

"Give Rog a hug for me, honey, and take one for yourself, too."

No gloom could overshadow the optimism that God had settled on Charlie today, not even Joyce's words. Something about Emily Cameron's personality changed his outlook on everything. She revived hope for a renewed life in him. Would she think him too forward if he would call her tonight? Or would it be too soon?

He made a quick stop at Boston Market for a potpie and creamed spinach to go then cut north to Manatee Avenue to head out to the beach. He loved this time of day. The snowbirds found their roost for the night, and he could get back out to the island without crawling along like a caterpillar.

A million stars and a fingernail moon scattered their light across the bay, giving the water the appearance of rolling tinfoil. He turned his head briefly to the right to see the view. Fishing boat lights dotted the sea like gems in a crown while the five-and-a-half-mile Sunshine Skyway shot like a comet from shore to shore in the distance. *It would be nice to share this with someone.* Emily's serene voice echoed in his head. He wanted to call her, but he had neglected to get her number.

He headed home and took the to-go box up to his refrigerator while he mulled over how to get in touch with her. She had his phone number, but that wouldn't do any good. She didn't seem the type to call men she hardly knew. He'd have to calm his intentions until tomorrow.

It had been a while since he dated anyone seriously. Hadn't he just told himself no one could replace Nancy? Perhaps that thought had been premature.

four

"Emily, who's in charge while you're away from the office?" said Linda.

Emily nibbled on the remainder of her energy bar from the day before. "You've been working as accountant for us for over three years. Don't you think Carson is the obvious choice?"

Linda closed the steno notebook and stuck the pen through the coils. "He's trustworthy. I don't think you'll have to worry at all. By the way, I've jotted down a few things I want to go over with you. Are you game?"

"No, ma'am. My only work while I'm here is to meet one client in Bradenton. Other than that, I'm on vacation."

Three hairpins dangled from Hattie's pinned-up ponytail as she drifted out of the bedroom. "Good for you, girl. I heard that." Hattie yawned. "You two do know it's Saturday morning, right? So why are you all up so early? Any coffee?"

Emily crumpled her wrapper and threw it in the trash. "No, and I'm dying for a cup. We have to go get that and a few other groceries before we let the morning get too far gone. How'd you sleep?"

"I would have slept fine except for Linda snoring in the next room. Tonight, I'll close my door." Hattie winked at Linda.

Linda moved to the lanai door and slid it open. "That snore was my release after being in airports for so long yesterday. My bed was great, Em. How about yours?"

"Except for a few random bumps here and there, it was

fine. Anyone game for hopping the Manatee County Area Transit trolley down to the Publix store? Shouldn't take us more than five minutes to get there. We can scurry back and head for the beach."

Hattie dropped onto the La-Z-Boy. "I'm game for waiting for you all on the beach."

Emily chuckled. All Hattie had talked about the last three weeks was lying in the sun. Emily lifted the purses from the dining room table. "Here you go, girls. Let's move. The sooner we get there, the sooner we can get back."

"Give me a minute to fix my hair and throw on some shorts." Hattie hurried into the bathroom.

Linda slipped a cup of water into the microwave and set the timer. "How was your trip in yesterday, Em?"

"Unusual." Emily had moved past yesterday's ridiculous notion that perhaps she could entertain having another man in her life—sometime.

"Emily? Look at me. What happened yesterday?"

Emily walked into the kitchen and leaned against the counter. "I actually met a very nice gentleman. He was very attractive, but his gentleness was what won me over. I feel as though I've known him for some time."

An overabundance of fancy-smelling cologne preceded Hattie to the kitchen. "He who? What are you two talking about?"

The bell dinged on the microwave and Linda took her cup out. "It seems that all of our good intentions are bringing forth fruit. Emily has met a man."

☙

Charlie was glad he waited until today to contact Mrs. Cameron. He wouldn't seem so much like a stranger with evil intentions this way and could drift down the beach and look for her without seeming like a stalker. If he found her, they'd talk. If he didn't see her, he'd head back home.

An airplane overhead flew a banner across the sky, announcing to someone named Allison that Benji loved her. His feet sunk through the thin membrane of wet sand to the dry sand beneath as he walked from the front of his house to the shore. As he headed past a clump of sea oats, he tuned in to the music of the waves and dodged partial holes and sand castles remaining from someone's fun the day before. Then he calculated how far away her condo was. He knew he'd never make it that far. Instead, he put his shoes on and drove to the public beach, which was about halfway between his place and hers.

He tipped his hat to the side of his face to shield his eyes from the afternoon sun and ambled in the direction of Emily's rental. Even though the chances were slim that he would see her, he eventually found her wading in the water with her friends. What a wonder that the pain of missing Nancy that had sliced his heart yesterday gave way to an explosion of infatuation today. He removed his hat and pushed out the words with barely a rasp. "Mrs. Cameron?"

"Mr. Parish. How surprising to see you today. Do you live on this part of the beach?"

Hattie poked Linda, and they both followed Emily as she walked up to the dry sand where Charlie stood.

Charlie's words caught in his throat. She seemed friendly enough. "I just live down the beach a jaunt. I thought I'd stroll down this way for a walk."

Emily gazed out over the water. "It's just so peaceful out here. I sat on the lanai last night and felt so close to God's creation. I wanted to get out here today so I could feel it again."

"It's a unique place. Were you able to find a good place to eat breakfast?"

"No, but we took the trolley to the store and rushed back so we could come down to the beach." She motioned to Hattie and Linda. "Let me introduce you to my friends. We all went to college together. This is Linda Warner. She works with me in Indianapolis."

Charlie shook Linda's outreached hand. "Glad to meet you, Ms. Warner."

"This is Hattie Lincoln. She's from South Carolina and occasionally makes it up to visit us in Indiana."

He nodded to Hattie.

Hattie responded with a welcoming smile. "Now, don't you dare call me Ms. My name's Hattie."

"I promise, Hattie." Charlie turned his attention to Emily. "How did you like taking the trolley?"

"I do like to walk, but the trolley came in handy this morning. I'm sure we'll use it again. How about you? Do you walk often?"

Suddenly exercise took on a new dimension for Charlie. "Well, to be honest, I used to walk and run all the time, but sometimes, circumstances change the desire for exercise. Now, I'm just starting out again."

A few threads of her bobbed, blond hair had a song of their own as they moved in the wind and glimmered in the sunshine. "Walking is second nature to me—a great stress reliever."

"Maybe we'll run into each other again." He lingered between anticipation and fear as a smile blossomed on Emily's face, and a rush of hope flooded his chest. *Ask her for her number, Charlie.*

Hattie nudged Emily in the arm. Charlie saw Emily's lips moving but heard nothing. Emily glanced back at Charlie. "We're heading back down the beach, Mr. Parish. Have a good day."

"Have fun." His words didn't match what he felt. Disappointment rumbled inside.

She turned and walked away while Hattie and Linda each motioned a hand in the air. He watched until Emily became a dot in the distance. He felt comfortable talking to her, although he'd have to take care not to let his eagerness show. While he'd hoped for more of a conversation with her, Charlie counted his blessings for being able to see her again.

He was captivated. Even though his time with Emily Cameron was short, thoughts of a new relationship hovered in his mind. A fresh vigor for life began to creep in on him as he got back to the public beach. There had to be a way he could contact her again.

In spite of bumper-to-bumper traffic on the way back to his house, the drive seemed short because thoughts of Emily filled his mind. If the opportunity came to see her again, he'd keep the conversation light and casual. No need to boast about the kind of lifestyle he had lived formerly as president of Southland Citrus Company. At that moment, he made the decision to keep his association with Southland Citrus out of the picture, at least for the time being. He wanted to be known for himself. Then, when the time was right, he would tell her how the Lord had blessed him over the years.

The third step from the bottom at his beach house creaked as he lowered himself to the cool wood, slipped off his shoes, and dropped them into the grass-covered sand. He'd not be selling his house soon. Things could be changing. Charlie Parish was breathless and not just from the walk home.

&

Hattie rolled her hair up into a hump on the top of her head and pinned it in place. "I still think you should have spent more time talking to the man, Emily."

"He is very nice, but I'm not here to meet anyone, Hattie.

Besides, if I believe that God has a plan for my life—and I do—then I won't have to resort to finding someone a thousand miles away from home."

Linda slipped her arms into a light blue denim jacket. "But Hattie's got a point. He seemed interested, and he was cute."

"I'll get my shoes. Discussion is closed. Now, do you two want to go to the Sandbar to eat?" While Emily finished dressing, her phone rang.

"Before you go talking, I'd just as soon snack here," said Hattie.

"Hi, Jen, how are you?"

"Mom?"

"Jen, are you on the island?"

"I just landed, and I'm looking for my shuttle."

"Do you know where to find him?"

"Him?"

"The shuttle. The driver is a very kind man from the island out here—at least mine was."

"I get a little discombobulated in airports I've never flown to before. Can you tell me where to go once I pick up my suitcases?"

"When you get down to the baggage claim area, the shuttle is supposed to wait right outside the west door. All the shuttles come to the same place. It's a white, twelve-passenger conversion van that looks more like a miniature school bus than a van."

"I think I see it. Does it say—?"

"Nancy Belle?"

"Yes, I see it. It has a woman driving it, Mom."

A quick thump rolled in Emily's stomach. "A woman?"

"Yeah, a woman."

"Is she young. . .old?"

"I can't see much beyond the tinted windows, but she

seems to be petite, has long hair tied back with a bandana, and past that, I can't tell anything. Why do you want to know?"

"Oh, no reason."

"You okay, Mom?"

"Sure, honey. Fine, I'm just fine."

"Okay. So, Mom, how long does it take to get to the island from here?"

"A little over an hour. Call me when you get close. The girls and I are deciding where to eat. I'll be back in time to meet you at the rental as soon as you get here." Frowning, Emily closed her cell phone.

"When's Jen coming in?" asked Linda.

"I figure she'll be here in an hour or two by the time they actually leave the airport. Anyone ready for some delicious clam chowder?"

"I love their grouper sandwiches at the Sandbar. Do you suppose we could order a light dinner there?" said Linda.

"Why don't we just go to the Beachhouse?" Hattie pulled the pins out of her hair and let it bounce across her shoulders. "It's nearly the same fare, but it's closer."

Emily shrugged. "Let's just go somewhere. I'm hungry. And I need to be back here when Jen arrives."

Just one little pin could let the air out of such a big balloon filled with hot air. Of course, the man probably knew many women. No, he didn't seem the type who would have more than one at a time. He didn't wear a ring that day in the shuttle. She forgot to look today.

Emily followed the others out the door as they headed for the restaurant. How long ago did he say his wife died? *Oh, Emily. You just told Hattie you weren't interested. You're getting yourself worked up over nothing. Do you really believe God has a plan?*

five

"Call him. He's dreamy. If I were you, I'd be pounding on his door right now." Hattie lifted her bagel with cream cheese from the peach-colored conch shell plate, broke off a piece, and slid it into her mouth.

Emily touched the ceramic mug filled with coffee to her lips. "I told myself I wouldn't dwell on the subject, so let's change it." The first two sips warmed her chilled body, and she let out a relieved sigh. Stan's ashes no longer intimidated her. She had allowed them to have far too much control over her for too long.

As far as Charlie Parish was concerned, she wasn't about to initiate anything. The past was in the past, and today was another day. For all she knew, he could be married to the other shuttle driver. Maybe it was a family business.

Linda leaned back in her chair and dangled her glasses between her thumb and first two fingers. "I say let's give it another day or so. He may not want to be contacted. You had to ask him for his card, right?"

Hattie touched Emily on the arm and sat down opposite her. "Oh Linda. Please don't counsel her to wait. She only has ten days, and he seemed interested when we saw him on the beach yesterday, right, honey?"

Emily closed her eyes. "You two are incorrigible. I can't even think about accosting the man. Some woman drove the van to pick up Jennifer. Maybe that was his wife."

Linda positioned her glasses on her face and leaned closer to Emily. "I'm just saying, play hard to get."

"She *is* hard to get, but she knows a good man when she sees him, and so do we. It's time for her to quit being so serious all the time."

Emily realized that no matter how much she tried to put Charlie Parish out of her mind, he still pushed his way back in. She pictured him standing next to her in the warm sand, just as he did yesterday.

Linda peered over the top of her glasses to Emily. "When's your business appointment?"

"Tomorrow. My tentative appointment's tomorrow. I have to contact Roger Parish again to make sure he's still willing to meet me on such short notice. He's a busy man. I called him from Indy, and he seems to be okay with it. I'll call him later to see if we're still on."

"Roger Parish? Wasn't Parish the name of the dazzling man we met yesterday? What if they're one and the same man?"

"Can't be related." Emily left the two sitting on the lanai while she headed for the kitchen. She dumped the remainder of her coffee and sloshed clean water around in the cup. "I'm putting this bag of bagels in the microwave. We'll draw bugs if I don't. This is Florida, you know."

Hattie followed her into the kitchen. She ran her plate under some water before she put it in the dishwasher. "Why can't they be related?"

Emily wiped her hands on the dishtowel and lowered her voice to a whisper. "He, Charlie Parish, is just your ordinary retiree trying to make a buck by driving a shuttle. Roger Parish must have millions. I mean, he owns a citrus company in Florida."

Hattie eased the dishwasher's door shut. "Why are we whispering?"

Emily motioned her head to the back bedroom.

"Oh, I get you. I forgot Jennifer came in last night. There must be lots of Parishes in Florida. Come on, Em. I say, do it. It's less than ten days before you go home. How often is a man like that going to land smack-dab in your lap?"

"I do have a reason to call him. I need to inquire if he knows about any boat we can take out to scatter Stan's ashes." Emily walked into the living room with Hattie following close behind. Linda joined them. Emily breathed deeply then opened her phone. Nine o'clock. She pressed in the area code then Charlie's number. Feeling Hattie's breath on the back of her neck, she walked out to the lanai. Before she pressed SEND, she stared at the phone. It shouldn't be that hard to make a call.

Charlie Parish's docile character could bring stability into her hectic life. What would it hurt for her to contact him? It wasn't for pleasure, anyway. It was for business. He'd tell her if he didn't want to help, wouldn't he? The fairy-wing flutter moved inside her stomach. It hadn't stirred her for years, but she remembered the glorious feeling. Her thumb opened her phone again, and she dialed his number.

He got it on the first ring. "Morning."

"Oh, um, Mr. Parish. It's Emily Cameron. I'm sorry to bother you, but I have a unique question to ask, and I felt perhaps you could answer it better than anyone else." She wrinkled her brows at Hattie and Linda who stood at the door, giggling.

"I'd be glad to help. What is it?"

"Well, this seems rather silly."

"Nonsense. My father always told me there were no silly questions. The only silly one was the one not asked."

She knew that. His mellow voice melted any apprehension she'd had about contacting him. "Sounds like you have a wise father."

"Had a wise father. He passed on to heaven just before Nancy did."

"Nancy?" Emily nearly bit through her lip.

"Nancy was my wife. She passed away two years ago."

"Forgive me. I had no right to pry like that."

"Don't worry about it. You have a question for me?"

Come on, Emily, form your words. "My daughter and I wanted to find passage out into the Gulf for a few hours, and I thought maybe you could head me in the right direction. Do you know of any excursion companies around?" *This was dumb, Emily. Why didn't you just look it up in the phone book?*

"I can get you to someone. First, why don't you tell me the nature of your trip so I can direct you to the correct person? Are you going for pleasure, deep-sea fishing, or what?"

Emily wanted to tell him. A man who'd lost his wife would surely understand her need to go out there and do this thing that Stan wanted done. "I don't know if you think this is stupid or not, but I've a promise to fulfill to my departed husband."

"Mrs. Cameron, I'd be glad to help you. Is everything okay?"

"What makes you think something's wrong?"

"Your voice, it's different."

Hattie wandered back onto the lanai. Emily nudged her away then walked back into the living room. "Yes, everything's okay, but do you think you can help? I'll try not to bother you any more after that."

"You're not bothering me, Mrs. Cameron."

Emily planted her eyes on the urn sitting out on the lanai. "It's Stan's ashes."

"Stan?"

"My husband, my former husband. It was his wish to have his ashes scattered over the Gulf. That's one reason why

I came down here."

"I'm sorry. That must be difficult for you."

"Yes. It is. Anyway, I'm just not sure how to go about this whole thing of scattering."

"I'm just heading into church right now. Why don't I pick you up afterward and take you out there myself? I'll arrange for a yacht to meet us over in the bay. Would two o'clock be okay?"

Emily sank into the chair. *What was I thinking? He's at church. I lost track of time. He probably thinks I'm a heathen.* "If it won't be too inconvenient for you, I'd appreciate your help. My daughter flew in yesterday and will be joining me."

"That's what we'll do then."

"Thank you, Mr. Parish. If you'll just give me the directions, we'll meet you somewhere."

"There's a marina close to Cortez Road. It's called Bradenton Beach Marina. I'll meet you at two o'clock at the dock near the office. Do you have a pen? I'll give you the exact directions."

"Just a minute." She held the phone away from her mouth. "Anyone have a pen real quick?"

Pouring a glass of juice with one hand, Linda used the other to motion to the dining table where two pens and a pencil rested upon a pile of brochures. Emily grabbed a pen. "Okay, Mr. Parish, I'm ready." She jotted down directions on a paper napkin, thanked him, and flipped the phone shut. As she joined the others, she wondered about the woman who drove the shuttle to pick up Jen.

Hattie pressed her finger against the opening on a bottle of foundation and tipped it twice before spreading the liquid over her sunburned nose. "Hey, girl. Look at me. What'd he say?"

Emily recalled her days at Butler when Hattie and Linda

had hovered over her much as they were now. They both had helped Emily through those early college years when she balanced being a young mother, still living at home with her parents. More than once, they'd planned dates for Emily, and more than once, she'd refused, based on her already faltering life. Nothing had changed with those two, and she still didn't need two sidekicks calling all the shots.

As she was about to reveal the conversation, the back bedroom door landed against the wall as Jennifer shuffled out. "Good morning, everyone." About three inches taller than Emily, Jennifer wore Capri jeans, a black Purdue sweatshirt, and a Cubs baseball cap. "I'm ready, Mom."

"Shall we go with you?" Hattie dropped her foundation bottle in her purse and pulled out a smaller bottle containing red nail polish.

Linda shivered at her last swallow of grapefruit juice. "Yes, I'm sure that's just who Emily wants tagging along, you and I."

"Sleep well, Jen?" Emily noticed Jen's frantic eye signals. She obviously wanted no part of Emily's two friends following. "Thanks for the offer, girls, but I think Jen and I should do this alone. You two enjoy your day, and I'll connect with you later. Keep your phones on in case I need to reach you."

"So, appease my curiosity," said Linda. "Is this handsome gentleman we met yesterday going to go with you?"

"What handsome gentleman, Mom?"

"He's the shuttle driver. They're talking about the shuttle driver. We happened to run into him on the beach."

Hattie loosened the lid on her polish. "This is private, right, Em?"

Linda sat down next to Hattie. "Oh, I know it's private, but I just wondered if he was going along."

Emily retrieved the urn, then settled it down into her

straw purse and surrounded it with tissues. She nudged Jennifer and motioned her head to the door.

Hattie stopped the door as Emily was closing it. "We still have time. Don't lose hope."

❧

Emily and Jennifer waited for the trolley at the MCAT sign near the condos. While Emily moved her hand around the bottom of her purse, looking for the napkin with the directions on it, Jennifer cooled off by waving her envelope-size purse in front of her face. "What are you looking for, Mom?"

"I think I left it on the table. I wrote the directions down on a paper napkin, but it's too late to go back. Here comes the trolley."

They took a seat facing sideways near the front of the trolley. Jennifer patted Emily's arm. "We'll find the place. It can't be that hard."

"I'm glad you're along, honey. Maybe we could ask the driver."

Jennifer pointed to the sign on the bulkhead of the trolley above the window. "It says don't talk to him while he's driving, Mom."

"Oops, didn't see that."

"Why are they carrying on so much about Mr. Parish? Do they think you can't find someone in Indiana, if you really want to?"

Emily pulled her bottom lip between her teeth. "I think we need to get off."

Jennifer pulled the yellow wire to ring the bell, and the trolley pulled up to the next stop. After they got off, they waited for a lull in traffic then darted across the street. "Do you remember any of your directions, Mom?"

"He said he'd meet us near the office." Multitudes of cabin cruisers, yachts, and passenger boats crowded the docks. They hurried along for a block until they got to the police station. "Jen, where's the driveway for the marina?"

"Looks like we'll have to cut through, Mom. The actual entrance looks to be several blocks on the other side of the police station." Jen took her mother's arm. "Come on. Watch the ruts in the dirt on this hill."

The bay breeze lifted the light odor of fish scales and gasoline fumes to Emily's nose as they walked to the marina. The sun beat intensely, penetrating through Emily's icy yellow blouse and white slacks. "Aren't you hot in that sweatshirt?"

"A little. I didn't know it would be this warm in March. I thought we came to Florida one time in March, when I was a child, and we saw snowflakes."

"We did see them, but that was up in the Florida panhandle in February."

This weather suited Emily. The Indiana winter had lasted far too long. She found herself wondering if Carson would be up to being in charge of the consulting business for an extra week. The more she thought about it, the more she wondered if she could get to know Mr. Parish a little better.

"Let's just stand here at the entrance, Mom, until he sees us, or we see him."

Emily stopped, closed her eyes, and then lifted her face. "Jen, don't you just love this sun?"

"Did you use sunscreen? You know how fair skin can burn in fifteen minutes down here." Jen pulled the bill of her Cubs baseball cap down over her forehead.

Emily raised her voice over the sound of a boat idling toward them. "Forgot." As she opened her eyes, she recognized the man driving. He raised his hand in a quick wave as he shut down his engine. "Mrs. Cameron. What a surprise to hear from you today."

"Mr. Parish?" Dressed in white trousers, a peach Hawaiian shirt, and Panama hat, Charlie Parish looked like he just stepped out of a tropical fashion magazine. *That smile must be inherent with him.* "That's so thoughtful of you to bring us a boat."

He squinted from the sun and smiled. "This is simply the means to get you out to a bigger boat. This must be your daughter." He circled a heavy rope around a mooring post then stepped to the dock.

"Yes. Charlie, this is my daughter, Jennifer. Jennifer, this is Mr. Parish."

Charlie shook her hand. "Are you both ready to go to the *Trinity?*"

Emily motioned to his boat. "This boat looks good enough."

"A boat like this is much too small to head out into the Gulf. The waves are too unpredictable." He stepped back into his boat and secured the back of it to the dock.

"They are?"

Nodding, he reached out his hand to her. She motioned for Jennifer to take her other hand until they both stepped down the stairs and were secure in the boat. "Who does the other boat belong to?" asked Emily.

Charlie pointed to two orange life preservers. "Please slip those on, ladies. We'll head on out the intracoastal waterway." He loosened the ropes and turned his boat around. Guiding his boat behind the wake of a large sailboat, he followed him under each drawbridge then turned toward the anchored *Trinity*.

"The crew will see to it that you are provided with whatever you need. The *Trinity* has everything."

"I don't need anything special."

His stare shifted from Emily to Jennifer. "Everyone

deserves to be treated special at one time or another."

"My mom certainly does." Jennifer embraced her mother briefly then linked arms with her. "So, Mr. Parish, you're the shuttle driver who drove my mother out to the island from the airport, Friday. I rode over here with Caroline Parish. Are you related?"

Emily felt the thump in her stomach. *Mrs. Parish?* Now her curiosity was aroused. *How long would the woman's identity be a deterrent to Emily?*

"That Ms. Parish would be my niece, Caroline. She won't work at her father's organic grocery store, but she'll drive a shuttle. She's trying to pay off her bills from the University of Florida."

Emily kicked her emotional self and warned her imagination to calm down. "I'm glad you've offered to help us out today. I just want to get this finished."

Jennifer leaned against her mother. "I'm not in a hurry. I came down here to say good-bye properly."

As the *Trinity* came into view, Emily's mouth dropped. "That, I assume, is the *Trinity?*" She and Jennifer looked at each other and then back to the yacht.

Charlie maneuvered skillfully up to the side of the *Trinity* where two ship hands dressed in white shirts trimmed in blue stripes caught the ropes he tossed to them. They tied them onto the yacht as Charlie crossed over. "Give me your hand, Mrs. Cameron. I'll help you up."

In one hand, she held the purse with the urn inside, and the other hand locked with Mr. Parish's. It seemed disloyal. Emily tried not to think about the tenderness of his touch, but she dared to let her eyes connect with his for a moment. They looked deep brown with green flecks—different in the sunlight. "How big is this yacht anyway?"

Charlie leaned his hand on the rail. "It's about two hundred feet by thirty-five feet."

"Mom, I just thought of something. When we sat down and talked about this with Jared and Jason, you mentioned you would confirm the regulations. Have you made sure this is legal?"

As Emily nodded her head, Charlie motioned to the stairway that led to the second level. "After you, ladies. Just to settle your minds, I know, for a fact, you are safe in scattering those ashes. The ship will travel out to the officially authorized distance before you proceed to your goal."

Emily pressed her fingers into her pounding temples and stretched her neck. As Charlie led them through a marble-covered formal entryway to a private sitting room on the middle floor of the yacht, she dug in her purse for an aspirin. He motioned for them to go in. "You two may use this room to talk out your plan for the day. If you need anything, there's a button to push on the side of the credenza. That will alert me."

Emily pulled an empty hand from her purse and nodded as Charlie exited the room. She would do everything she could to make this occasion momentous for her daughter. She knew Jennifer would try to do the same for her. One way or another, Stan would find his final resting place today, and Emily could move on with her life.

six

Charlie hadn't been this nervous since his first date with Nancy. Emily Cameron called him for help. At least, she felt comfortable in asking him. Did he even dare think that Mrs. Cameron would give him the time of day?

To busy his mind while he waited for the ladies to do what they came to do, he meandered through the yacht, checking in on his professional crew, cluing them in to the fact two newcomers were aboard. He stepped inside the captain's bridge where the computerized technology made steering the ship a simple task. "What's the weather look like this afternoon, Robin?"

The young man in charge of guiding the yacht darted his eyes from one instrument to another. "Not good, sir. Looks like a storm is brewing and likely to reach land around four this afternoon."

Charlie moved around behind him to check the readings. "Bad one?"

"No, sir, not bad by Florida standards. The ladies might have a problem being out here though, especially if they're inexperienced sailors."

"Go ahead and start the engine. Let's move out while they're talking. If they're not finished with their conversation in time to beat the storm, we'll turn around. Nevertheless, I want to get this done for Mrs. Cameron. I get the feeling she needs to take advantage of the time she has. If they decide to abort when we're out there, that's their business."

Charlie knew how she must feel. How do you say that final

51

good-bye? As long as there were things around to shout at you, your loved one's loss could dictate your entire life. Until yesterday, he didn't think he'd ever be able to give up Nancy's memory. Then Emily Cameron stepped on his shuttle. He had to admit a spark of hope ignited something in him when she called earlier.

Robin put the ship in motion. "I'll have us out there in a few minutes, sir."

Charlie gave him a salute then dashed up another flight of steps to the upper deck where a good friend worked at setting out a buffet for lunch. Charlie stuck out his hand. "Ted, how's it going?"

Ted lowered a pile of dishes to the table and gave Charlie a questioning look. "I need to ask you the same question. How's it going, and is that young woman the lady you told me about at church?" He positioned three crystal goblets at precisely the same point for each place setting on the table.

"That's Mrs. Cameron's daughter—her married daughter. Didn't you notice her wedding ring?"

"No, I'm talking about the other young one. Did you say her name is Cameron?"

Charlie narrowed his eyes. "Emily Cameron from Indiana. I met her on Friday in Tampa."

Ted ran his finger around the edge of each charger before he set them in place. "In Tampa? Where, the mall? A restaurant? New in town? You didn't tell me why I was to keep your identity secret."

"She came over on my shuttle."

"She looks like a keeper, Charlie."

Charlie nudged each knife on the place settings until they were equal distances from the spoons. "I can't let my emotions get tangled up with someone who is here on vacation—and a short vacation at that. I drive her back to Tampa on Sunday."

Ted wrinkled his brows. "Man, if you don't jump on this opportunity, I know men who will."

Charlie waved him off. "Steady, Ted. Neither one of us knows the woman well enough to think about anything other than friendship."

Ted chuckled and set a china plate on each of the chargers. "Are you moving forward on this charade thing you told me about a month ago, where you dress down and pretend not to be rich? Is that why you didn't want this lady to know?"

"People on the island already know who I am. Even so, I'm not telling Mrs. Cameron anything unless she asks. She's fresh, unassuming, and doesn't seem to focus on those things. For now, I'm not revealing anything."

Ted eyed Charlie. "So, let's set up a scenario here. What if you two decide to have dinner or something? You're not worried she'll find out your former citrus-king identity?"

Charlie looked away. "The waves are beginning to pick up."

Ted sat down and motioned for Charlie to sit. "Okay, so you don't want to talk. She won't be here that long. It's probably not even an issue."

Charlie ignored Ted's invitation to sit. He laughed as he turned to head back downstairs. "You're right. It's probably not even an issue, at this point. See you later." After descending the circular stairway at the back of the boat, Charlie walked into the master quarters next to the dining room. He wiped his finger across the mahogany-stained metropolitan table, smiled, then relaxed into the deep seat of the canvas sofa. Tess had cleaned the boat after all. His own house didn't sparkle this much.

He had often thought about quitting the business he was in, selling the house, and escaping on his boat. It would be adventurous. His grandkids would like that even better than coming to the beach house.

He hadn't been daydreaming long before Ted knocked on the

door then cracked it open. "Charlie, I'm afraid it's getting too windy up on top to do the luncheon. Since I don't want to take a chance getting stormed on, I'm going to move everything down to the dining room."

Charlie sprung to his feet and peered out the side window to the black-gray clouds choreographing with the angry sea in the distant west. "You're not kidding. The ladies are in the dining room talking. Can you move it in here? There's plenty of room."

Ted raised two fingers to his forehead. "You're the captain."

Charlie pushed him out the door.

Caution made a sudden circle in Charlie's stomach as he prayed Mrs. Cameron and Jennifer would make a quick decision. If they couldn't come to an agreement soon, they'd have to go out another day. He wouldn't mind that. It would give him one more chance to see Mrs. Cameron, but he had the feeling she needed to act today.

❧

The atmosphere in the formal dining area tensed as Emily and Jennifer sat across from one another. Jennifer's downcast eyes drew words of comfort from Emily. "This is the best time to do it. You know that, don't you?"

Jennifer blinked. "I'm ready, and I'm not ready—know what I mean?"

"I know exactly what you mean. We have to move on, though. Dad never meant for us to stare at the urn for the rest of our lives. He has known what he wanted ever since he first stepped on Bradenton Beach."

"I don't think that bothers me as much as something else that happened. I felt a little sad when you took down all his pictures from the wall. It looked like you didn't care about him anymore."

The revelation came without warning. Emily extended her hand and covered Jen's. "You haven't seen what I've done with them. It was going to be a Christmas surprise for all of you children, but I'll tell you now to ease your concern. You know how artsy Linda is. She's dividing all the photos into four groups, along with loads of snapshots I've collected over the years, and creating beautiful scrapbooks, one for each of us."

"That's awesome, Mom. I love that idea."

"I think Dad would like that, too."

"He would, Mom."

"You know how much Dad loved you."

"He adopted me, Mom. That says it all. I never knew any other father's love except Dad's love. You had always compared it to how God adopted us into His family."

"And adopting you was Dad's idea."

"Mom, you've always been honest with me, but I've never actually been ready to listen to you on this issue. Whatever happened to my natural father? Did he ask about me? Did he disappear? What happened?"

Emily hadn't anticipated Jennifer's asking about her father today. "I can say this. We were very young people when I became pregnant."

Jennifer's shoulders dropped. "Is that all you want to say?"

"Jennifer, help me here. I'm trying." All Emily's years of social restraint relating to her past waited to tumble out. She interlaced her hands on the table in front of her and sat at attention. "I camouflaged my pregnancy from people in my town as long as I could before my mother and father sent me to live with my aunt near Chicago. When my mother realized I wasn't about to give you up, she moved us back home."

"I knew that."

"Wait till I finish. By that time, my so-called boyfriend had disappeared, along with his family."

"You really don't know where he is? I thought you made that up." Jennifer's tears spilled over her lids.

"He was young and. . ."

"So were you, Mom."

"He didn't 'get it.'"

"You did. You carried it alone. How dare he leave you to do that alone?"

Emily squeezed Jennifer's hands. "I didn't do it alone. Even though I made some very bad choices, God helped me when I asked for His forgiveness. My mom and dad supported me in my final decision. Besides, we all had a new little bundle in our lives, and we grew stronger because of you."

"Mom, I'm sorry for all the times I doubted you on this issue. I'll never ask again, and I'll never stop being grateful for what my dad, Stan, did for me. He loved me for myself, just as God does. I never knew any different. I belonged to both you and Dad, and, after a while, got two brothers in the deal."

"Speaking of Dad, are you ready, honey?"

"Just one more question. After we do this, will you go with me back to Indiana?"

Emily pushed away from the table. "No, I won't. I'm on vacation down here. I need the rest, and to be honest, so far I'm enjoying myself."

"I've seen the way you and Mr. Parish look at one another."

"Do we look at each other a certain way?"

"I can cancel and stay down here. I took the entire week off work."

"Don't." Emily took Jennifer's hand in her own. "You have to let go of me as well as Dad. I appreciate your concern, but I'm going to be okay. Hattie and Linda are taking good care of me."

"They're a little wild, don't you think?"

Emily teased her with a wink. "You know they only have my best interests at heart. Besides, who knows whether I'll finally rub off on *them*. Now, Mr. Parish has been so gracious to get this boat rented for us. Let's not take advantage of him any longer. Let's say good-bye to Dad."

≈

While the mega yacht began to pitch with the swelling water, Charlie tapped the tips of his fingers together. He wanted to know her better, yet he didn't want to pretend to be someone he wasn't. *You have to be up-front. She won't be here that long.*

Charlie stared out the window again. He doubted they could stay much longer in the growing surf. At the same time, he saw Mrs. Cameron and her daughter walk across the deck in front of his window. He hopped out of his chair and out his door to signal their attention. "Ladies, I hope you don't mind us casting out to sea. As you can see in the west, there is a storm on the horizon. We're in a good position right now for you to get everything done."

Emily rubbed her hands up and down her arms then took hold of the railing. "The wind's already picked up something fierce, hasn't it?"

"We'll be okay for now, ma'am. Would you like a coat to put on?"

"No, I think I'll be fine. Let's get this done."

"Are you ready?"

Jennifer put her arm around her mother's shoulders. "Yes, Mr. Parish. We're ready. Where's the best place for us to stand to scatter my father's ashes?"

"It's too windy on the top deck. I recommend you stay right on this level, but go to the opposite side of the boat."

Emily's eyes drifted to the rolling waves. "Okay, come on, Jen. Let's do this."

Charlie followed a few feet behind then fell back. Mrs. Cameron seemed to be doing fine with the daunting task ahead of her, but he well knew what it was like to say good-bye. He watched from behind a rescue boat as she held the urn, and Jennifer removed the lid.

Emily said something to Jennifer then Jennifer nodded to her. Charlie directed his attention away. He waited there until he heard them approach from behind.

Jennifer supported her mother by her arm. "You look a little green, Mom. Are you sick? Here, let me carry the urn."

"It is getting a little rocky out here. Get me below."

Charlie shot into action. "What can I do for you, Mrs. Cameron? Can I get you something to drink?"

She barely moved her head. "No, just get me back to shore, Mr. Parish. It's already been quite a monumental day. Let's not top it by me getting sick."

Charlie led Emily and Jennifer into his private quarters where an exquisite candlelight luncheon table, set with aquamarine plates resting on apricot-colored chargers, awaited. He knew he could count on Ted.

Emily's eyes gaped. "What's all this?"

"The cook insisted on treating you ladies to lunch while we head back to shore. Do you feel well enough to eat?"

Emily dropped into an overstuffed chair. "I don't think so, I'm sorry."

Jennifer laid the urn in her mother's lap and pulled out a chair. "Well, I will, Mr. Parish. Thank the cook for thinking of us. It's been a while since I've sat down to a lovely meal such as this. Mom used to cook all the time on Sundays and. . . By the way, will you be driving me back into town to catch my flight, or will Caroline?"

"Let me give her a call. She just lives in on the mainland. I'm sure she'll be more than willing to pick up a few extra bucks, especially if she gets to drive her father's Mercedes out to the island." He left the room for a few minutes then switched the overhead light on as he came back in.

After a quick bow of her head, Jennifer took the pleated

apricot-colored napkin from the coquina shell ring and spread the cloth on her lap. She nudged the gold-handled fork into the chunk of escargot and sliced through it with a knife. As she tucked a bite into her mouth, she groaned. "This is delicious, Mr. Parish. I wish Mom could enjoy it."

Emily shook her head.

"I'm so thirsty." Jennifer tipped the gold-rimmed crystal goblet to her mouth and took a big gulp. "Were you able to get a hold of your niece, Mr. Parish?"

"I did. She'll meet us at the marina. I'd say another half hour would do it."

"Thank you so much for taking care of that. I'll have no time to spare. Mom, are you sure you don't need me to stay?"

Emily shook her head and waved her hand over her shoulder. Charlie walked over to her chair and stooped down in front of her. He positioned his hand on the armrest. "Mrs. Cameron, I don't feel right about letting you just sit here. Are you sure you're okay?"

Emily nodded her head. "Thank you, Mr. Parish. I just think I'm feeling the letdown from the stress of knowing I had to do it but didn't want to do it. I'll be okay."

Jennifer patted her lips with the cloth napkin then sat in a chair next to her mother. "My mother never was one to go out on boats. My dad wanted to take a cruise one time, but Mom said she'd be more comfortable where the land was firm."

Emily pinched the bridge of her nose. "I think I'd try it again, Jennifer. Just not when the waves are so high."

Charlie wanted to touch her arm, to reassure her that whatever she felt, God could help her get through it. While he wanted to wrap his hand around hers and offer his help in any way that he could, he realized her seasickness overruled any other activity. "We are almost there," he whispered as his eyes tried to find hers.

seven

Emily teetered a little after Charlie helped her onto the dock. "Thanks so much. I think the solid land will help me get back to normal."

He gestured to Caroline who stood in front of her father's Mercedes in the parking lot. Emily released her hand from the warmth of Charlie's then grasped Jennifer's arm.

Her daughter's eyes filled with concern. "Call me if you need anything."

Emily gave a quick nod then hugged Jennifer. "Good-bye, honey. Don't worry a thing about me."

"I'll let you know when I get back in Fort Wayne." She broke away in the face of Caroline's urgent pleas to hurry so they wouldn't be late. Emily waved a good-bye to Charlie, then hurried up the hill, across the highway, and down to the trolley stop. As she waited and watched the storm clouds grow closer, she contemplated walking. *Do I really want to ride a trolley after my unpleasant experience with the rocking boat?*

As sprinkles of rain hit her face, Emily made her decision to go it on foot. While the walk turned out to be farther than she thought, she got under the safety of the parking garage at her condo just as the thunder echoed across the water and the rain really let loose. Mumbling a quick prayer of safety for Jennifer who'd be riding to Tampa then flying home, she hurried up the stairs and punched in the code for the key.

Once the door closed behind her, not even the pounding rain disturbed the silence. She nearly gave in to the temptation to sit and enjoy it. However, she walked out onto the lanai and scanned the beach for her friends. It wasn't hard to identify Linda's red beach dress and Hattie's yellow straw hat with two plastic gardenias.

Two men carrying beach chairs followed her friends up to the condo. The strangers' gallantry stirred Emily's thoughts of Charlie. *Charlie Parish, you have been so kind today. I don't think I even told you.* Emily closed the sliding door, grabbed a couple of towels, and scurried to open the outside door.

Hattie shimmered with rain dotting her oiled skin. She pressed her hand against Emily's forehead. "Em, you look green around the edges with a tinge of sunburn. Are you okay?"

Emily handed her a towel. "I'm good now. Who were those men?"

"I don't know. They offered to carry our chairs, so we took them up on it," said Hattie.

"Did you enjoy the sun?"

"What there was of it, I did. By the looks of things, you got more than we did."

"Jennifer chastised me for not wearing sunscreen."

"How was the ride?"

"Hattie, I've discovered something today. I don't think I'm cut out for long-term cruising or sailing. I'm made to have my feet firmly on the ground."

Linda waved off the men at the bottom of the stairs then turned to Emily. "Sounds like one of your spiritual quotes, Em."

Emily shoved a towel into Linda's hands. "Very funny."

Hattie took the chairs from Linda and set them inside the door. "There's nothing wrong with terra firma."

"Girls, dry off and sit down," said Emily. "Let me tell you about my trip."

Linda pushed on the door, ruffled a towel through her hair, then followed Emily and Hattie into the living room. "I was just about to ask you how things went with Jen."

"They went as well as could be expected. Jen asked me about her father, again. This is the first time she's ever really heard me. I think she always had this romantic notion that there was more to my story than what I told her. I believe she finally had closure today."

Hattie swiped the towel across her arms. "It's about time she realized that her elusive birth daddy didn't stick around."

Emily's tone mellowed. "Mr. Parish was very nice to us today."

Hattie wrapped her arms around Emily. "He's perfect, Emily."

"He was very gracious to us. You would have died to see the yacht he took us out on. The cook laid out a superb meal for us. It was a shame that my seasickness kept me from enjoying it."

"You could have a yacht like that if you wanted to," said Hattie.

"I don't want to spend that much money on something like that."

"Where is Jen now?" asked Linda.

"On her way home. Caroline, Charlie's niece, took her back to Tampa in her father's Mercedes."

Hattie shook her head. "I wish I could have seen that yacht."

"Let's just see where we can go to eat and forget about boats and Charlie Parish, for now." Emily kicked off her tennis shoes then headed for the dining area where a folder filled with menus from the local restaurants lay open on the table. Hunger rolled in her stomach. A light breakfast and no lunch left room for a nice dinner. What was that place where she and Stan used to go?

Linda and Hattie joined her, and all three of them leafed

through the brochures and menus. Hattie pounced first. "Hey, this place just south of here sounds good." She laid the opened menu on top of all the others.

Emily glanced then continued leafing through the offerings. "That's where we went yesterday. I still love their clam chowder."

Linda pulled a menu out of the mix and opened it. "How about this rib place? The note on the menu says the meat falls off the ribs, it's so good."

Emily took the menu from her. "Probably not tonight with it raining so heavily. The inside might be filled, and we don't want to sit outside. Here's a cute little café-type place. Oh, Hattie, they have your favorite—duck. No, what was that other place? Fast Eddie's. They had the best onion rings. That's where Stan and I used to go." Emily fanned through the phone book to see if Eddie's had a number. "I wonder if they've closed. I can't imagine that, but it has been a while since I've been here."

"Here's one for the Beachhouse, again. The food is delicious. Let's just go back there," said Linda.

Emily headed for her room. "Fine with me. I'll hurry. I want to shower before we go." Emily freshened herself and then rummaged through the clothes she had brought. While her idea had sounded good in theory, she couldn't bring herself to wear only the casual outfits. Instead, she decided to mix and match her nice clothes with them. She dressed in her favorite fashion jeans and donned the red polo shirt from Walmart—a good combination.

As she revolved the blow-dryer around her head, her eye caught the glimmer of her wedding rings. Her finger would feel bare, but she wanted to remove them. She had taken that first step to say good-bye, and now she must continue freeing herself from other links to what once was. Emily removed her rings and stashed them in her makeup bag before she joined the other two.

Hattie wore black, pencil-tight pants and a blue, sequined tank that revealed more skin than Emily wanted to see. Her gold serpentine chains hung down, one inside and one outside the tank. She stood at the door. "Are you going to change your shirt, Em?"

"No."

"You're wearing that?"

Emily gave her friend the once-over. "I could ask you the same question about that tank top."

Linda emerged from the bedroom in her oversized floral shirt in shades of black, blue, and purple. Shell earrings in the same color palette dangled to her shoulders. Navy bell-bottoms hung to the floor. "Hattie, you're beautiful, except for the skin. Get a sweater or something to cover it. Emily, are you wearing a different shirt? Come on, you have something better than that to wear."

Emily widened her eyes. "Girls. I have a confession to make." She paraded out to the living room and plopped into the brown rattan chair.

Linda pulled one up beside her, but Hattie hovered with hands on hips. "What's your confession?"

"I've decided to change my style while I'm here. I didn't have the courage to tell you before—but Linda, you'll appreciate this—I went online and bought some clothes at Walmart before I came."

Hattie shook her head, spritzed her Chanel into the air, and then walked through the cloud of mist. Her body dropped hard to the chair at the dining table. "Change your style? Have you gone mad? Why would you want to do that?"

Emily shrugged. "I've been in the spotlight ever since I married Stan. Don't get me wrong. I've thoroughly enjoyed it, most of the time. I've been blessed. I've had abundance. On the downside, I've put myself on the line for everyone to criticize and even more so after I took Stan's position. Sometimes, I've felt that people want to know me because I'm successful. I want to be accepted for who I am and not for what I have. Is that so wrong?"

Linda wrapped her arms around Emily's shoulders. "No, but I just can't believe you've done this. This is so out of character, that's all. I can't imagine you shopping anywhere but the best stores. Nevertheless, if you want to do it, then go for it."

"Thank you. Now, why don't you two go ahead without me while I think about this. I'll come in a few minutes."

"So it sounds like you're still not sure what you want to do. Why do you want to come alone?" said Hattie. "We'll wait."

"But Linda has a point. Hattie, let me think through this. You know me. Maybe I'm making my situation worse by trying to be someone I'm not."

Linda hugged her then pulled Hattie out the door. "Sounds confusing to me. We'll see you in a few minutes, Em. We'll go ahead and snag a table at the Beachhouse."

Emily walked back to the bathroom, plugged in her flatiron, and focused on the imprint from her rings. She popped the lid on her hand lotion, squirted a small puddle into her thirsty hands, and tried to massage the imprint away.

After she smoothed her hair with the flatiron, she stared at the reflection in the mirror. While she had closed a chapter in her life, relief came, but loneliness also vied for her heart. Perhaps it would linger like the imprint from the rings had.

Emily unplugged the iron and turned out the light. A sudden clap of thunder while she put on her sandals made her realize she wouldn't be walking anywhere tonight. She hurried to the lanai door and drew it open with the intention of standing on the lanai to watch the storm pelt the beach. But wind-driven rain made that impossible. After she latched the door, she walked back to her bedroom.

It had been a while since she had opened her Bible. Perhaps this was a God-given opportunity to meditate on His Word for a while. A slightly molded spot in the bed creaked and sunk in when she sat down to read. The Bible's pages, well worn from years of use, spilled out words to her heart. After a while of reading and focusing on passages she had underlined over the years, she felt Him speak to her. *Trust in Me, Emily. I love you for who you are.*

Thank You, Lord. Help me remember those words. She laid the Bible down and peered out the French doors to her balcony. After a day or two of rest, she'd meet with Roger Parish and work on gaining his interest in her consulting services. Her mind flitted to Charlie. How remarkable that two men from two completely different backgrounds, who just happened to have the same last name, would impact her life in ten days' time.

As the reflection of the setting sun brightened the sky, she turned to leave the room and head for the restaurant. The mirror caught her image, and she stopped to look at it and brush a few hairs from her face. With an earnest gaze, she searched beyond the woman in the mirror. Maybe her lack of direction in her personal life was an issue of her heart. *Am I seeking someone else's approval and not Yours, Lord?*

❧

"Will this table be okay, Mr. Parish?" The hostess placed two sets of silverware wrapped in paper napkins across from one another on the table.

"If the weather channel didn't put a 70 percent bet on rain, I might sit outside. I think the forecast might be right, though. Look at those threatening skies."

"You'll probably be safer in here by the window. Enjoy your dinner. Your server will be with you shortly."

Charlie positioned himself facing the entryway then acknowledged the waiter. "That was fast service!"

"You got here before we got too busy. Can I get you something to drink?"

Charlie pulled his shirtsleeve back and glanced at his watch. *Laura's usually on time.* "I'm waiting on someone, so maybe I should wait before I order anything. She should be here any moment."

"Would you like a cup of coffee in the meantime?"

"That would suit me fine."

Charlie waved to a church friend who sat with his family of five across the room. When he looked to see if Laura had shown up yet, his attention was drawn to the stunning woman with the blond highlights who had just entered the restaurant.

Emily Cameron's face was aglow from the mixture of the afternoon wind and sun. The crisp color contrast between the red polo and denim fashion jeans set her apart from every other woman in the place, and her demeanor suggested she felt much better than she did earlier. He pushed away from the table and stood to wave at her, just as Laura walked in from the opposite direction.

"Hi Charlie. You didn't know I'd come from the beach, did you?"

"Laura. Glad you could make it. Here, sit down." He stood to assist her.

"Thank you, sir." A quick smile dusted her face.

"Would you care for anything to drink? I'll signal the waiter."

"How about a glass of iced tea?"

"He convinced me to order coffee."

"I'm plenty warm from being in my garden today. I just soak up the sun so quickly."

The waiter answered Charlie's signal. "Are you ready to order?"

"No, not yet. The lady will have iced tea." Charlie glanced back to the entrance. He drummed his fingers on the table when he realized he'd lost sight of Mrs. Cameron.

"What's up, Charlie?"

"I thought I saw someone I know."

Laura threw her head back with a giggle. "Charlie, you seem rather nervous tonight. Is everything okay?"

"I'm being foolish; I'm sorry. How was your day?"

"I spent my morning in the garden. There had to be a million bugs out today. When Morgan was alive, he usually took care of the bug problem for me."

He hardly noticed she was talking as Emily Cameron's aura once again captured his attention. Another couple standing near Emily had entered into a conversation with her. When she laughed, her hand rose to her face and covered her lips.

He looked back to Laura. "He was a good man. I'm sure you miss him as much as I missed Nancy."

"Nancy. She was a gem. She and I had such lovely times together. I miss her, too."

As hard as he tried not to, Charlie's attention drifted to Mrs. Cameron again as she browsed the racks of souvenir shirts. Before Charlie knew it, she pivoted and headed out the door. If only there were some gracious way he could get across the room and get her attention before she left.

"Laura, would you mind if a friend joined us?"

She scanned the entrance. "Not at all. He or she?"

"A lady I shuttled from the airport on Friday. I think she's alone."

"I'd love to meet her. All three of us 'alone' people can commiserate together."

Charlie excused himself and made a beeline toward the door. As he squeezed through the gathering crowd to find Emily, she had already disappeared. He headed back to his table and arrived at the same time as the waiter.

He set a plate of pineapple bread on the table. "You folks ready to order now?"

Charlie wiped the sweat from his brow. "Laura, what may I order for you?"

"It looks like she disappeared. Do you want to go find her?"

"No, let's order."

"I can order for myself, Charlie. I'll have a refill on my iced tea, and please bring us an appetizer of calamari. I'll have the seafood au gratin for my meal."

Charlie pulled his gaze away from the door. "I'll have a bowl of soup. Doesn't matter what, just bring me something."

The waiter scribbled on his order pad. "Clam chowder or black bean?"

"Just bring me the chowder, thanks."

Charlie unwrapped his silverware and began adjusting their positions. After that, he wiped each one with his napkin.

"Charlie, are you okay? You seem so preoccupied tonight."

He shifted in his seat and folded his hands in his lap. "Laura, I've wanted us to sit down and talk."

She lifted her glass to her mouth then set it down. "So have I. Do you want to go first?"

He lined up his silverware then monitored her face as he continued. "I don't think we want to talk about the same thing."

She touched his hand and matched his gaze. "Then let's not talk tonight, Charlie. Let's wait until we have more privacy."

"This isn't. . ."

The waiter had come back. "Here you go, one iced tea, one chowder, and the calamari is coming. Sir, are you ready to order your main course now or do you want to wait?"

Charlie looked up at the waiter. "I'll wait a few more minutes, thanks."

"Okay, I'll stop back to take your order."

After Charlie prayed for their meal, Laura filled him in on her day. "Did I tell you all three of my cats are expecting kittens?"

Charlie dipped his spoon into his chowder, tasted it, and then set the spoon on the table. "Laura, I don't know how to be delicate about this, but I'm not sure what you're thinking about us. I don't want to hurt you or anything, but I don't see our relationship progressing anywhere past friendship."

Laura stiffened in her chair. "Thank God, Charlie. The way you've been shuffling around in your chair and playing with the silver, I thought you were going to say just the opposite."

Charlie clasped his hands together on the table. "You've been a friend for some time, but other than that, it's simply not there for us."

"Charlie, you didn't hear me. I am more than happy to keep our relationship right where it is. I don't think of you in that way, either. I just want us to be friends and keep our separate lives."

"No kidding? What a relief! I guess I must have misread something."

"Seems as if we both did. I guess we were made to be BFFs forever."

Charlie chuckled. "Sounds good to me."

Another glimpse of red in the crowd drew his attention. Emily had walked back into the restaurant. The hostess led her in his direction. He combed his fingers through his hair.

Laura followed his gaze to Emily. "Charlie, you look like you've seen a ghost. Is that your friend?"

He looked at Emily just as she turned her face in his direction.

eight

Emily cultivated unimaginable scenarios as she wondered what could have happened to Hattie and Linda. They said they'd meet her here, didn't they? Apprehension seized the moment when her eyes fell on Charlie Parish sitting with a woman at the table next to hers. She quickly composed herself and gave him and the lady with him a nod of acknowledgment. She had to admit, she was a bit undone at seeing him for the second time today—and with another woman.

He stood as she sat at her table. "Would you care to dine with us? Laura and I would love for you to join us."

Emily held up her phone. "Actually, I'm waiting on my friends. They were going to meet me here, but I can't seem to locate them."

Laura smiled. "I'm sure they're okay. People are pretty safe out here on the island. Is there anything we can do?"

Emily scanned the faces of the crowd waiting for seats. She shot Laura an absentminded nod. "I'm just hoping they'll call me soon."

"The offer still stands. If you change your mind, please feel free to have dinner with Charlie and me."

"Thank you." She hid her face in the menu, trying desperately to bring her thumping heart under control. Did warmth automatically radiate from his smiles? How did he manage to make her feel so at ease yet so upended? Then she felt a hand on her shoulder.

She stood and put her arms around Linda. "I've been worried about you two. What happened?"

Linda pulled out a chair. "We decided to head back and wait with you. We must have walked right past each other."

"I'm so relieved you're all right. Where's Hattie?"

"She's coming. Believe it or not, she decided to change into something more presentable. Seems your good morals have been rubbing off on her." Emily and Linda both sat down. Linda unrolled her napkin and spread it on her lap. "Isn't that charming man sitting at the table behind us Mr. Parish?"

Emily leaned across the table and said softly, "They invited me to join them, but I declined."

"Why are we whispering?"

Emily rolled her eyes then spotted Hattie. Her black long-sleeved knit top with silver seagull decals drew several compliments from patrons in the restaurant as she made her way to the table, stopping first at Charlie's. "Mr. Parish? Remember me? I'm Hattie, Emily's friend."

Charlie took her hand as he stood. "I remember. This is my friend, Laura."

Hattie switched her hand from Charlie's to Laura's. "Glad to meet you. How cozy that we're all here together. Laura, this other lady is Linda, and, Laura, did you meet Emily?"

Laura nodded at Linda then smiled at Emily.

"Enjoy your supper." Hattie sat down between Emily and Linda, facing Charlie's table.

"Whatever happened to you, Em?"

"Linda and I figured we passed each other when you two doubled back."

"Who is that woman with your man?"

Emily clamped her hand down on Hattie's arm. "Shh. He says she's a friend. Now, let's just leave it at that and order. I'm just about spent for one day. And, for your information, he's not *my* man."

After dinner, Hattie and Linda strolled out to the beach while Emily stopped at Charlie's table. "It was nice to meet you, Laura. Have a good evening. You, too, Mr. Parish."

"Maybe we can get together for dinner some night while you're here," suggested Laura.

Charlie gave a quick nod. His wink provoked Emily's hand to rush to her stomach. "That would be nice. I'll talk to you later." Holding her breath, Emily made her exit. Once outside the restaurant, she inhaled two deep breaths of air.

Only a margin of moon remained to flash in and out of the on-again-off-again storm clouds as she hit the beach and minced across the damp sand. Laura had been more than cordial at inviting her to join them for dinner some night. Would that be possible? Hattie waved to Emily from the water's edge as Emily's cell phone vibrated against her thigh. She moved it to her ear and plugged the other ear.

"Emily Cameron, here."

"Mrs. Cameron? This is Roger Parish returning your phone call."

Emily leaned the phone away from her face as she cleared her throat. "Yes, Mr. Parish. I've been wondering if we're still on for our meeting on Monday."

"I'm sorry to get to you so late, but I can meet you at ten o'clock on Tuesday morning instead. Will that work for you?"

"Ten o'clock it is."

"Do you know how to get here?"

Emily drifted toward Hattie and Linda. "Yes, I've been on the mainland many times. Besides, I did a MapQuest before I flew down here. It shouldn't be too hard to find."

"I'm looking forward to discussing your services. I think you can save us a lot of money."

"Okay, then, I'll see you Tuesday morning."

"Good-bye, Mrs. Cameron."

Emily shut her phone with a surge of victory and thrust it back into her pocket as she joined the others.

Linda was ankle-deep in the water. "Come on and wade. It's refreshing."

A shudder moved through Emily's body. "It's a strange mixture of tropical mugginess and chilliness out here. I should have brought a sweater."

Hattie slipped off her sandals. "Linda, I think it's a little cool."

"It's fine after you get used to it."

Hattie sat down in the sand and wiped the bottom of her pants across her wet legs. "Let's take in a movie."

Emily stooped next to her. "You're going to get wet sitting there, and there are no movies out here on the island. We'd have to go into town, and we have no transportation. You'd have to carry me back, though. I'm so tired."

"What's with this island?" said Hattie.

"It's private—just the way most people out here like it."

Linda stretched a hand to Emily. "Here. Let's call it a night, then. Tomorrow's another day."

Emily's attention was drawn to the laughter from the couple walking in their direction. "Isn't that Charlie and Laura?"

Hattie sprang to her feet and brushed the wet sand from the back of her pants. "Is that Divine Providence or what?"

"No, it is not. Now, mind your manners."

"You know I'm a romantic. One never knows."

Linda nodded in agreement. "She may be right this time, Em. They're walking right to us."

"We meet again." Laura strolled over to Emily. "Would you ladies like to join us for dessert at my place?"

"We sure would," Hattie drawled.

Between flying in on Friday night and spending the afternoon getting sick on a boat, Emily was ready to call it a day. "I think that would be wonderful for my friends. But I'm going to head back to the condo and climb into bed. May I take a rain check?"

"You may." Laura nudged Charlie with her elbow. "Why don't you drop Emily at her place, and I'll take Hattie and Linda in my car?"

"Wonderful," said Linda. "See you in the morning, Em. We'll come in quietly."

Hattie and Linda chattered as they followed Laura to her car.

Emily froze. "Did they all secretly know each other and plan this?"

Charlie chuckled. "Laura watches out for me." He looked up at the sky. "It's finally clearing. Looks like we'll have a dandy of a day tomorrow."

Emily's head spun with the swiftness of the evening's plans. Hattie and Linda had abandoned her. And here she was. . .alone with Charlie. "I hope you don't feel pushed into taking me back."

He held his arm out. "Not at all, Mrs. Cameron. I'm a tad weary myself. Your friends and my friend make a good trio. I'll see you home then scurry home myself. That is, if you'll agree to join me for lunch tomorrow."

Emily kept an acceptable distance between herself and Charlie but rested her hand in the crook of his elbow. Glad for the darkness that hid her nervousness, yet pleased that he had shown her this courtesy, she accepted. "Lunch would be wonderful as long as you call me Emily. Tell me when and where, and I'll meet you there."

"Let's meet down where Manatee Avenue heads into the main beach, and we'll decide where to go from there."

"Fine, I'll be sitting under a Coca-Cola umbrella."

He chuckled. "Every table there has a Coke umbrella."

Emily let go of his arm as soon as they got out of the sand

at the parking area. "How did you ever come to the decision to be a shuttle driver?"

"I wanted to do something that kept me in touch with people yet allowed me the freedom to be outside the four walls of a typical office. My brother is an idea man and is always coming up with these unique plans to make money. When he proposed this one to me, I jumped at the chance. I wanted the liberty to talk to people about God, life, and their perception of how the two come together. My brother does the business end."

"What a fun job, Mr. Parish."

"The name's Charlie."

❧

Steam veiled the double doors that led into the gym on the mainland. Why Charlie ever allowed Ted to talk him into this exploit boggled his mind. He leaned on the door and moved inside then found Ted waiting at the coffee bar.

"Hey, Charlie. How're you doing?"

"Okay, I'm here. Where do I start?"

"Charlie, I see that look of mistrust on your face. Don't worry, my man. I know it's been a while since you met me here once a week back when I was in finance. Remember that old saying, 'This is the first day of the rest of your life?' Come with me. We'll drop your stuff in a locker and head for the elliptical."

"I'm not sure I'm ready for that."

"It will be better on your feet and heels than the treadmill. It's the best place for you to start. It burns fat faster."

Charlie frowned at Ted's Cheshire grin. "Oh my. Why don't I like the sound of that?"

"From what you told me last night when you called, the amazing woman you have a date with is enough motivation for you to start back on this program."

"Since Nancy died, I haven't had the heart to come work out here without her. But I have been walking." Charlie patted his stomach. "Guess I do have a few pounds to drop and a belly to firm. Let's get started."

Ted, who worked out here on a regular basis, moved ahead of Charlie, directing him toward a lineup of ellipticals and treadmills. Charlie was convinced his coordination and the elliptical would clash. Six of the machines already oscillated faster than Charlie ever thought he could go. He draped his towel around his shoulders and started to get on an empty machine.

"Move down to the last one. I'll take the one next to it."

Charlie whipped the towel off his shoulders and wiped the moisture from his already sweating face. "Are you sure about this? There are three empty treadmills in the front."

"Come on. I remember the day you almost bought one of these machines to put in your home."

Charlie plunked his water bottle into the holder, grabbed hold of the sensor area of the handlebars, and straddled the bar on the support stand. Imagining a million eyes on him, he looked to his left and right to find the riders engrossed in whatever played on their earphones. As he eased his right foot onto the right pedal, his weight caused it to revolve enough that the left pedal knocked him in the bottom of his shin. "It's been a good year since I've tackled this thing."

Charlie positioned his left foot on the other pedal as Ted's muffled laugh drew his ire. "It's been way longer than a year, Charlie. These are all new machines. You can choose a workout or simply push the START button. It's automatically set for thirty minutes."

"I'm able to handle that."

"Okay, but I think that's too long for your first haul. Push the down arrow and set it for ten minutes."

"Ten? I could easily do twenty." Charlie yanked the bottle out of the holder and sloshed some water into his mouth.

"Trust me, Charlie. I wouldn't steer you wrong."

"I insist, Ted. Now that I'm back in the swing of things, I know I can do this."

Charlie grabbed the upright handlebars that pulled his arms in a rowing motion in direct rhythm with the pedals. It felt unnatural, but after about fifty revolutions, he began to get the timing right. Ted pedaled twice as hard as he held to the stable sensor bars.

Charlie focused on the weather channel playing on the flat-paneled screen in front of him. As the local weather appeared on the screen, he noticed his heavy breathing. "Time to stop, Ted."

"Hey, man. Not as in shape as we thought, eh?"

Sweat beads rolled down Charlie's crimson cheeks as he dismounted the elliptical. "This was a good idea, Ted. Nevertheless, I should have done the treadmill. I'll be lucky to make it to the beach."

"We just got started." Ted pointed to the free weights.

"Not now, Ted. I need to get this crick out of my leg and fast." Charlie stretched one leg out straight and bent from the waist. "Ah, that feels good."

"So, you had a nice time last night?"

"I'm meeting her for lunch on the beach today."

"No kidding? Maybe Roger will get this retirement home stuff off his mind now."

Charlie switched legs. "Roger only wants what's best for me. He thinks that living alone on the beach is too stressful for me since Nancy died. He'll relent, after a while. But I have no plans to tell Rog anything, yet. I'm just getting started."

"You don't have much time. You'd better sweep Mrs. Cameron off her feet quick."

nine

Light filtering through the French doors flickered across Emily's face. She had waited all night for morning to come, waking up nearly every hour. She rolled to her side and felt around underneath her bed for the quilted clutch purse she stashed there the night before. She pulled out her compact, flicked it open, and wiped the loose powder from the mirror. *My, I don't feel as old as I look.*

Did last night really happen? Using her feet, she shoved the bed coverings until they lay bundled at the foot of the bed. Then she got out of bed and tiptoed down the hall. A shiver worked up her spine as she trekked across the linoleum in the kitchen and retrieved the bag of coffee from the microwave.

The rich aroma of the special blend prompted her to add an extra scoop of coffee into the filter. As the coffee dripped, she leaned her elbows on the countertop and peered through the opening to the living room and out the lanai window. She never expected to be at such a pivotal point in her life at her age, nor did she ever expect a suitor to knock on her door again. It was the furthest thought from her mind, yet here it was.

Before long, Hattie scuffed across the hallway floor into the kitchen. "Emily? You're such an early bird. Only that divine aroma could have awakened me this morning. I told myself I just had to get up and enjoy a cup with you."

Emily embraced Hattie then pulled two oversized mugs from the glass cupboard. After she filled each with coffee, she poured the remainder in a carafe. "Hattie, it's after ten.

I didn't even get my walk in. Come on, girl. We have some talking to do."

Hattie raised her brows. "Last night?"

"Yes, ma'am, last night. My rational brain doesn't know how to process what's happening to me, Hattie. Grab the coffee cups, and I'll take the carafe."

Hattie pointed to the refrigerator. "Don't forget to grab your milk, honey."

They barefooted to the lanai then eased the sliding door closed. Emily shivered as the steel on the sliding door rubbed across the bits of salt and sand that had lodged in the runner.

Hattie set the cups down on the table then flipped the damp cushions on the chairs to the dry side. "Isn't it gorgeous out here, Em? I think I could easily move down here and take up golf or something like that."

Emily poured the coffee as Hattie sat down. "And leave your business behind?"

Hattie held the mug to her lips. "Wouldn't you?"

A smile perked while Emily sat down. "If I didn't know any better, I'd say I was tricked into spending time alone with Charlie last night."

Hattie leaned forward. "Oh my, are you puttin' me on, girl?"

"It would be easier if I were. It was rather obvious you and Linda willingly cooperated with Laura to get Charlie and me together."

Hattie bit her bottom lip. "How did it go? Did you spend a lot of time together?"

Emily poured some 2 percent into her coffee, turning it light beige. "We did just what we planned. He took me back to the condo and said good night."

Hattie patted her hand. "At our age, honey, you better do everything quickly."

"Hattie."

"Tell me exactly what happened."

Emily blew across the coffee in her cup. "We talked for a while at the beach then he brought me straight home. He is one of the kindest, gentlest men I think I've ever met."

Hattie maintained eye contact. "What about that candle?"

"What candle?"

"You once told me no one could hold a candle to Stan."

Emily's cup clicked as she set it on the glass table. She pulled her feet up under her. "I think Charlie represents something different from what Stan was. Stanley was fiercely competitive, realistic, and insistent upon perfection. I loved all those things about him. I don't know everything about Charlie, but I do know from our short visits he's not afraid to dream, he seems to be able to take life as it comes, he has a handle on where he sees himself ten years from now, and money doesn't control him. I love that."

"Honey, can you live with that last one? You have money and he doesn't."

"I can tell you I didn't get much sleep last night." Emily crossed her arms and stared out over the Gulf. "I'm just going to enjoy the fact that a man has asked me to dine with him, and he's not doing it to gain recognition or riches."

"Dine with him? When?"

Emily looked at her watch. "Oh my—in about an hour. I better get ready."

"Time for dreams to come true."

"Hattie, I don't know if I want to dream yet—not about that. This is the tropics. You have to be careful down here, make sure you're not allowing yourself to fall for atmosphere."

Hattie dribbled more coffee from the carafe. "I would love to have a little joy from the atmosphere. I can tell you this. When we had dessert at Laura's house, she said that Charlie sure seemed to be preoccupied with you at the restaurant."

Emily walked back into the condo. She had noticed that Charlie often glanced her way. While she enjoyed the notion that someone might be interested in her, she thought she might be misreading his signals. "Then I'll pray, Hattie. I'll pray that I'll know beyond a shadow of a doubt if Charlie Parish is meant to be more to me than a lunch date."

❧

I'm not going to rush into anything or sweep her off her feet. What was Ted thinking? Emily and I are merely having lunch together. Charlie approached the outside café at the public beach. The seagulls' sharp hawks filled the salt air as they jockeyed for position to collect food from unsuspecting tourists. He spotted Emily sitting at a table on the south end. She was dressed in a yellow blouse and white pants. Her white straw hat had a yellow polka-dotted ribbon traveling around the crown.

A warmth of emotion traveled through him as he drew near to the attractive woman. Emily Cameron seemed to materialize out of nowhere on Friday. He'd thought he'd be picking up an old spinster at the airport. Instead, he found her. He now was faced with the fact that everything he had been missing in his life might be found in the woman sitting a few feet from him.

Her radiant glow lifted his heart. He'd hardly slept the night before, but the vision of this woman energized him. He had a woman—his equal—to share time with. She was the type of woman he could marry someday. *You're getting way ahead of yourself, Parish.*

He thought her smile was just for him when she spoke. "Good morning, Charlie."

"Morning, ma'am. Could I interest you in lunch?"

"Sir, do you have my best interests at heart?"

He melted at her teasing. "Only the best." He screeched the chair across the sand-laden cement and sat across from her. He felt as comfortable as he had with Nancy. His natural inclination would be to take Emily's hands in his. Nevertheless, he forced himself to be patient. If anything was to be, they'd both know it. He didn't want to scare this beautiful bird away.

She adjusted her hat. "I think we chose a perfect day for lunch here."

"I think you're right." He smiled, hoping she didn't notice him continuing to work out the cramp that still grabbed at his thigh.

"Do you want to do lunch now or go for a walk first?"

"A walk would be fantastic."

She pushed her chair away from the table before he had a chance to help. "I'm ready, Charlie. I'll drop this cup in the trash on the way by. Should we head north?"

"If it's okay with you, let's walk down to your condo. Would your friends care to join us for lunch?"

"I don't know if they'd agree. They think that they've matched you and me up for some special date."

"So does Laura. She called this morning to make sure I had taken advantage of any opportunity to ask you out."

"You know, this peaceful rush of the surf, the warmth of the sun, and the gulls harking overhead are all lulling me into this tropical experience. You're very blessed to live here."

"I am." He started moving toward the water and she followed.

"So, did you tell me you live up the beach?"

"Near the north end."

"So you know your way around well."

Charlie hustled to keep up with Emily's fast-paced walk. "You might say that."

"Born and raised here?"

He rubbed his thigh and glanced at her. "Born and raised in Winter Haven. After my folks passed on, I moved to the coast."

"Do you have children or grandchildren?"

"Two sons. One lives here and the other lives in California. Two teenage grandchildren. How about you?"

"I have two sons and Jennifer. You met her." She cast a knowing look in his direction.

"I enjoyed meeting her." Charlie forced the words out through his short breaths. He stopped suddenly and pointed out over the water. "We might see dolphins if we wait a while."

Emily repositioned her hat. "Where?"

There was rarely a time when he looked out and they weren't there. Now he needed a rest. He hoped, with all his might, they would break the surface of the water. Before long, a gleam shimmied along the peak of the waves. "There." He pointed out to the horizon. "There they are."

"How beautiful. I wish we could see them closer." She touched his arm. It calmed him, but it also awakened a little more within him. One of her weekends had already passed. Today was Monday. Could he convince her to spend all her remaining days with him?

&

"Charlie, forgive my curiosity about so many things, but where do you go to church?" A quick rush of heat flicked through her body as she wished she could pull back all the words that just hurried out of her mouth. What difference did it make? She was only going to be here for another few days.

"I'm glad you asked." He picked up a stone and tossed it into the water. "I go to a church on the north side of the island and have been there for more years than I care to admit to. I first gave my heart to the Lord when I was eighteen."

"Did you meet Mrs. Parish there?" She edged into their walk. Again, she chided herself for letting too many of her private thoughts form into words. Maybe he preferred not to talk about it.

"No, I did not. We met in college. I was dating her sister, but we didn't hit it off very well. Then she introduced me to Nancy."

"Nancy Belle. That's why the stencil on the door of your shuttle. What was she like?"

"Nancy was my equal in every way. We were very much alike." He sighed, then continued. "She was a wonderful mother to our two boys. They miss her very much since she passed on two years ago."

"I know what you mean. Stan was a great father, even to Jennifer." It slipped out before she could stop it. He didn't need to know about her recklessness in her high school years.

"'Even to Jennifer'?"

Emily took a deep breath. *Well, here goes nothing.* "I don't know whatever happened to her natural father. We were young. Fifteen to be exact. I was sixteen when Jen was born. My parents had me in church and everything. I just rebelled against them and God and went my own way." It seemed the pang of guilt would never go away.

He stopped and turned to her. Her eyes were drawn to his because they filled with empathy. "Why is it when we're young, we think we have the better answer? If only we had listened to our parents' wisdom and warnings."

"My parents had never thought I'd make a mess of my life. They didn't know what to do with the whole situation. They wanted to protect me from embarrassment and themselves, I imagine. I had a favorite aunt living near Chicago. They decided to send me there until I had the baby. They expected Aunt Mary to put everything in motion to have the baby adopted. When they finally accepted the fact I wanted to keep the baby, they relented and brought me back home, where we all dealt with the situation together."

"But even though you made some unfortunate choices,

you stayed true to your sense of right and wrong. You didn't compound the situation. I admire you for that. I'm glad you kept her, Emily. That must have been a tough decision."

Emotion washed through her as her eyes filled with tears. "I'm so sorry, Charlie. I don't know what's gotten into me. That was so long ago. I've moved on."

Charlie moved his arm around her shoulder and they continued their walk. "Sounds like you haven't."

Come on, Emily. Where's that corporate spirit? Do or die. Nothing will get you down again. Never. Her body thundered with unresolved feelings, but she managed to curb her tears and breathe herself into a state of denial. "I'm okay, now. I don't know where that even came from. Let's just walk."

Sinking into the curve of his arm, Emily willed her feet to move. Although desperately embarrassed, she found herself wanting to pour out more. She sucked in what remained of her dignity and dabbed her eyes with the back of her knuckle.

Charlie broke the silence. "Did Jennifer get home okay?"

A laugh of relief came as she pulled away from Charlie. "Yes, yes, but I wouldn't put it past her to fly back down here. She's worried I can't do life apart from Stan or my kids. Jen was already eight when I married him. She saw how our love drew us together to the point we were nearly inseparable."

"I understand that. My son and daughter-in-law in Bradenton are the same way. They don't understand that I'm capable of moving on. I have a lot of years left." He laughed.

For the first time, she wasn't afraid to look him in the eye. Something about his nature encouraged her to drop her doubts and fears and befriend him. She hoped he felt the same way. "Charlie Parish, I believe we have a lot in common."

As naturally as one would hug a friend, he situated his arm around her shoulders. The welcome touch of a friend brought her close to Charlie's side. They both broke the embrace at the same time. "I believe we do, too, Emily." His hand found hers as they continued down the beach.

ten

"Where do you recommend we eat, Charlie?"

Charlie had a quick flashback. Nancy would have said the same thing; she had always deferred to his choices when it came to restaurants. However, he knew her palate and often chose one of her favorites. "We can walk to almost anywhere. There's food for every appetite."

Emily drew her hand away and rushed in front of him to escape an approaching wave. He caught the scent of her freshly shampooed hair. "I love anything." She moved away from the shore as she pointed to a low-breaking wave. "You're going to get wet shoes with the next one."

Charlie processed the message just as the incoming tide washed over his right foot. He sidestepped toward Emily. "Too late!"

Emily giggled.

Even her laugh is as fun-loving as Nancy's. How long can I keep comparing Emily and Nancy?

"Better walk up here where I am." Emily extended her hand.

He grabbed it, satisfied with her touch, believing they had established a connection, wishing he could forget about how little time they had together. He gestured toward the distance. "Is that Hattie and Linda?"

"I can tell it's Linda by the way she pokes her hair up into her baseball cap." Emily waved.

"And Hattie?"

"Hattie never looks the same two days in a row. Emily motioned to the woman wading near the shore.

"That lady has long hair."

"As I said, Hattie is always changing."

"You all seem so different. What's brought you together?"

"We were friends at a local college I attended in Indy. Since then, Linda and I have worked together, and Hattie keeps in touch from South Carolina. They insisted that I come with them on this trip."

"What kind of work?"

Linda waved as she walked toward them. "So what's this dreamy look on your face, Em?"

"It's simply a look of pleasure at being able to be outdoors in the warmth." Emily dropped Charlie's hand and folded her arms. "Charlie wants us all to have lunch together. Are you two free?"

"We were going to go find a way down to St. Armand's Key in a little while. Let me go see if Hattie wants to do lunch, instead."

Charlie studied Emily as she waited for Linda. He wanted to have lunch with her, then dinner, then breakfast tomorrow. How much of her time could he monopolize without taking her away from her other plans? "Emily, may I ask you to dinner tonight? There's a beautiful place on the beach I'd like to take you."

Emily squinted and shot a glance at him. "I'd like that. I think Hattie and Linda had planned on a movie in town tonight, but I'd rather have dinner out here."

He repositioned himself so she wouldn't have to look into the sun. "Wonderful. I'll pick you up at six."

"Why don't you tell me where the restaurant is, and I'll meet you. As you've heard, we are going to take in some shopping while we're here. Hattie and Linda will be more than glad to make sure I get to the right place."

"It's called the Beach Bistro. If you take the trolley, you'll have to go to the north end of the island first where it turns around, then back to the restaurant. It'll take you about thirty-five minutes or so. It'll take you about thirty-five minutes or so. I think the best solution is for me to escort you."

"I'll be fine, Charlie. Can you bring me back to my rental, afterward?"

"I will."

Hattie pulled her hair back, twisted it, then fastened it with a barrette. "Why don't you and Charlie go ahead for lunch? I'm going shopping."

Linda shrugged. "I guess I will, too."

Charlie stifled a laugh at Emily's helpless look. "Emily, shall we just meet for dinner tonight instead of going for lunch?"

"You don't mind?"

"I don't mind. I'll see you then."

"Thanks for understanding."

❧

Charlie stopped by the Beach Bistro on Gulf Drive to double-check his reservation for dinner. When he pulled into the lot, he decided it would take less time to phone them. He loved the atmosphere here at night. A special restaurant for a special occasion. *A red rose in the center of the table set with a white tablecloth. A table facing the beach to watch the sunset. White-glove care from all the waiters. Delicious food. She'll love it.*

Next, he phoned Roger.

"Hey, Dad, how're you doing?"

"I'm good."

"I just hung up from a phone conference with 'the Lion.'" Roger chuckled.

J. T. Sparks, the young entrepreneur from a competing company, had jokingly become known as a jungle cat because he had stalked his prey and quickly become the head of his organization. Now J. T. was stalking Southland Citrus and pushing for a merger. "He still wants to press you into a partnership?"

"Yeah, Dad. How did you hold him off for so many years?"

"I tried to put it in perspective. He's ten years younger than you, and I treated him like a son—a son who had to be told no, he couldn't have what he wanted. Also, I prayed a lot, Rog. Don't forget about keeping God in the equation. There's always an answer when you do that."

"Yeah, I know that. This is big business though, Dad. Sometimes I don't have time to stop and pray about every little thing."

Charlie's heart sank. Forty years of careful, loving teaching would eventually penetrate Roger's heart. He knew God would honor all the prayers he spent on Roger and his brother Dan. He knew the Word of God to be true when it came to training your children in it. Nancy had read the Bible to them every night and had kept them in church on Sundays even when Charlie was away on business. God would bring both boys around to a right way of thinking. They might have to learn some lessons along the way, but they'd come around.

"Gotta go, son. I'm taking the Mercedes into the car wash."

"See, Dad, if you'd move into town, you wouldn't have to drive so far. It's too bad there's no car wash on the island."

"The drive isn't that far. It's easier than doing it at the house. Good luck with J. T."

"Okay, Dad. Talk to you later."

Emily would be surprised, to say the least, when she found out what kind of car he drove. Perhaps it would be a good lead-in for gradually letting her in on his real life. After all, she seemed to care for him just the way he was. It would be nice for her to enjoy some of the fineries of life instead of living life at a low to middle income.

Cleaning the Mercedes out at this time of the week rated

as one of the most surprising things Charlie had ever done. Nancy had always been the one to take care of the vehicles.

Traffic crawled on Cortez Road on the way into the mainland. Once he got in town, he planned out his time for an afternoon of running errands before he stopped at the car wash. His tendency for tight adherence to schedules proved to be his undoing, though, as he headed back out to the island. An unexpected stop as the drawbridge opened on Manatee bit fifteen minutes from his day.

After a quick stop at home to shower and put on dress khakis and a Hawaiian shirt, Charlie headed for the Beach Bistro. He loved the elegant touch with valet parking—different from most restaurants on the beach. He greeted the people who waited inside for their reserved tables. Then his eyes fell on Emily who sat poised and serene staring out at the Gulf. He blotted the sweat beads that had collected on his forehead as the maître d' led him to the table.

She seemed entranced as the lightly rolling waves teased sandpipers into scurrying in all directions. A look of dreamy contentment filled her countenance. Charlie wasn't sure if he wanted to stand and stare at her for a while or join her.

Their eyes connected as he sat opposite her with his back facing the floor-length window. "Emily. I'm sorry I left you sitting here all alone."

She held her hand out to greet him. He held on tightly. "Why, I'm not alone, Charlie. Look at all these wonderful people joining me. I've had a lovely time conversing with the couple at the table next to me." Her quick smile assured him anger wasn't a part of her personality. He wanted to stand and pull her into his arms—give her a tender hug. Maybe later.

"Traffic this time of year is horrendous and unpredictable."

"All us snowbirds down here?"

"Yep."

She turned his hand slightly. "Charlie, what a beautiful watch."

"My son gave it to me as a gift. Kids these days. You never know what's up with them. Can you imagine he would spend so much money on a watch? He's settled himself into a good business."

"It's gorgeous. He must love you a lot." She ran her fingers over the band, and he captured her hand with his own.

"Tell me more about your children." Charlie moved his other hand into his pocket and tugged on the corner of his kerchief until it came out. He shook it open and blotted the beads of sweat from his forehead.

"Jared lives in Portland, Maine, with his wife, Amy, and my two grandsons. Jason, our twenty-four-year-old, still says he lives at home, but he's gone more than he's there. Well, I should say, he used to live on campus, but he moved home after Stan died. He was worried about his old mother. I must say he's been good company though. Jennifer is a policewoman. She and Paul have three girls. What about your sons?"

"My two boys are total opposites. The oldest is married with two kids and has his own business. The other one headed out to Hollywood to make a name for himself. He's been out there for ten years already and has yet to land a role. He works at some pizzeria at night and walks dogs in the daytime. He told me he's working on a screenplay or something. He once had a relationship with a girl named Penny. They had plans to be married, but she was killed in a boating accident. I don't think he'll ever find someone else."

Emily squeezed his hand and placed her other hand on Charlie's. "You know, it sounds like your youngest has a creative urge in his spirit. That's okay, Charlie. He may just prove he can do it. It takes time to be successful in the arts."

That's what Nancy always used to say, and now, Emily

confirmed it. Charlie's insides tingled with a new awakening. Something he never expected to happen played with his heart. "You may be right, Emily."

❧

Their engaging feast on slow-baked maple-leaf duckling had stretched from one hour to two. Even though they were nearly stuffed from the abundance of food, they decided to share a piece of mouthwatering, prize-winning key lime pie. At Charlie's insistence, Emily took the last bite. "This is so creamy. I love it. Thank you, Charlie."

Eventually, the waiter returned with the bill. Charlie paid then intertwined his hand with Emily's. Since her attention was riveted on the window, he turned to see the pinks and purples in the sky as they created a backdrop for the disappearing sun. He pondered what to do next.

He felt like a young teen falling in love. Nevertheless, being much older now settled the notion in his heart. He wanted to please God with every ounce of his being, and he didn't want to make any moves that would embarrass her. "Well, what shall we do next?"

"Do you want to go for a walk, Charlie?"

His legs felt like lead, and he was too full even to consider it. "Would you mind going for a drive instead?"

"I'd love to. Will you excuse me for a moment?"

"I will."

Emily smiled as she disappeared into the ladies' room.

When Charlie got into the men's room, he steadied himself against the sink. He'd been dizzy before but never like this. A quick pain darted through his arm but then subsided. After he filled his lungs with a couple of breaths, he doused his face with some cool water. As soon as he walked back outside the restroom, he acted as though he were okay.

After scanning the restaurant, he saw Emily walking out

the door. He hurried his pace to catch up to her. "Looking for me?"

"I wondered if you'd walked out on me, so I came out here to find you." She winked.

"Never." His voice felt shaky.

Her eyes sparked in question. "Never?"

Charlie looped his arm over her shoulder and led her across the parking lot to his car. He balked at his weird and wonderful feelings. "Does this seem strange to you?"

Emily clutched her straw purse and nodded. "It does, Charlie. I almost feel like I'm being unfaithful to Stan's memory."

"I feel unfaithful, too. I find myself wondering if Nancy can see me." He observed her reaction at seeing his Mercedes. Her face revealed nothing. He opened the door for Emily and held her hand to help her into her seat. He took a couple more deep breaths before he got into the car. "Have you been into town lately?"

She fastened her seat belt. "Nope, not this trip, but I will be tomorrow. I like your car, Charlie. So many people down here drive Mercedes. How come?"

Charlie inserted the key into the ignition and started the car. "This was Nancy's baby. What's tomorrow?"

"I'm mixing my vacation with a little business."

He waited for her to say more, but she didn't. "I'll take us into town then back again, just so we can see the bay. The stunning view at night will take your breath away."

"Sounds good, Charlie. Let's go."

Charlie clicked his belt then rolled down the window. Perhaps all he needed was a restful sleep. Once Emily was back in Indiana, he'd have his heart checked out, and what kind of business was she in, anyway? Why didn't she want to talk about it?

eleven

The sound of gunfire shot Emily out of bed. She stuck her head through the curtains to peer down into the street. Puffs of smoke coming from the tailpipe of a soft drink delivery truck set her mind at ease. As she sat back on the bed, her mind returned to her evening with Charlie. Just the touch of his oil-smooth hand on hers gave her the assurance someone cared.

She had never believed she could ever enjoy the delight of a love interest again. She felt almost as giddy as when she first fell for Stan. *Oh Stan. Would you mind?* She had originally hoped her meeting with Roger Parish later this morning would be a turning point in her life. Perhaps her date with Charlie last night was the real turning point.

Emily shoved her feet into her slippers and scuffed into the bathroom. Four splashes of cold water on her face helped eliminate the evidences of insomnia. As she blotted a hand towel across her cheeks, she admired the sun-blushed look. *Maybe skip the foundation this morning?*

Thinking better of it, she decided to save the experiment for another time. She had a business appointment to attend. Even so, she chuckled at her predictable routine for creating a flawless face each morning.

She dressed then readied herself for her presentation. Organizing her information for her meeting with Roger Parish proved to be a challenge. She last remembered seeing the flash drive on which her documents were stored on the bathroom counter at home. So she tweaked what she did have into perfection and knew she had the experience to wing it.

Time was creeping up on her. After she gathered her shoes from the bedroom, she tiptoed down the hall and made her way to the kitchen. She couldn't fathom starting the day without coffee. Nevertheless, she didn't have time to make it. As long as a ten o'clock headache didn't interfere with her meeting, she'd be fine with only the fruit and yogurt smoothie.

The produce in Florida just seemed to be better. She dropped a peeled banana, four heaping tablespoons of plain yogurt, and a peeled, whole orange into the blender, then pressed the button. The two dish towels she threw on top of it to shut out the intrusive noise didn't muffle any noise. Nevertheless, Hattie and Linda didn't stir.

Emily sipped from her glass on the way to the lanai door. The first sip cooled her throat and quenched her need for a healthy start to her day. She eased the door open a bit. Barely a whoosh sounded as each light wave made its way to shore. A balmy breeze tempered the inside air. She checked her watch. It was five till nine.

She slipped on her heels as a knock sounded on the door. As Emily went to answer it, Linda made her way to the kitchen. A young man at the door dangled car keys in front of Emily, spoke in broken English, and indicated that he'd wait at the car for her.

Emily was tempted to call the car rental service. She shot a glance to Linda. "Now what?"

"It didn't sound good, whatever he said."

"I better get down there."

"Can I go in town with you?"

Emily eyed the pajama-clad Linda. "I can't wait. What do you need?"

"I thought I'd find some fast food for breakfast, but I'll make do out here."

Emily went back into the kitchen, then picked up the blender and poured the remaining smoothie into a fruit juice glass. "Here. Once you get a load of this, you'll never eat fast food for breakfast again. Besides, the island is full of fantastic restaurants. Why don't you do breakfast on the beach?"

Linda lifted the glass to eye level. "Ugh. This looks rather sick. I think I'll pass."

"You're chicken. Anyway, I have to go. I'll have my cell. Call me if you need me to bring anything back. Have fun this morning."

"Yeah, you, too. I hope you get your account."

"I just want to get this account in the bag, then I have the rest of the week to relax."

Emily dashed down the steps with her leather tote hung around her shoulder, purse in the crook of her arm, and the handle of her briefcase clutched in her hand. The young man from the rental agency sat inside the car. When he saw her coming, he turned off the ignition, bounced out of the car, and babbled in broken English, "Sorry, sorry."

Her shoulders fell at the missing mirror on the passenger side of the Toyota. "What happened?"

"Sorry for car." He handed her an agreement—complete with a side note telling about the damage—which she promptly signed then handed back to him. She didn't believe in bad luck, but starting off the morning like this didn't seem very promising.

❧

The sun had just started peeking around the corner of Charlie's house and shone across part of the screened-in lanai. The day had started on a new note. Coffee didn't drip in his house this morning.

The memory of the terrifying physical experience from last night still had its talons in him. He'd heard that sometimes too much caffeine could bring on anxiety and heart palpitations.

A friend had told him that when he drank coffee, it sent a burning pain from his stomach into his esophagus and throat. Often, it traveled into his arm, just as a heart attack would.

It had taken Charlie three hours before he'd felt relaxed enough to try to go to bed. Now he knew it was time to get his diet in order. Whatever he ate or drank to cause that pain was not worth it. He had squeezed a half-dozen oranges into juice and sat on the lanai to drink it.

Emily Cameron's presence in his life settled him. She seemed to like him and had no clue about the blessing of wealth that rested on him. She hadn't asked, so he hadn't told. He'd let the rope out slowly to reveal who he was and watch for her reaction.

His cell phone vibrated on the rattan table next to his chair. It was Caroline calling.

"Hi, honey, what's up?"

"Uncle Charlie, I have a 102 temp. My mom's going to take me over to the clinic to get checked out. I can't do the run to the airport today. I apologize."

"Don't worry, honey. Call and let me know how you're doing later. I'll be praying for you. What time do I need to be in Tampa?"

"You have ten people arriving on Delta around eleven and two from the American flight around one. From my info, it seems the first family added a kid to their traveling party. You have twelve people besides yourself. I don't know how you're going to safely seat everybody."

"Let me worry about that one. We've done it before; we can do it again. Now you take care of yourself, and I'll take care of our travelers. Love you."

"Love you, too. Thanks."

Charlie finished the last of the juice and locked up the

house. Putting twelve people into eleven leather captain's chairs could get tricky. In addition, he never liked making one group of people wait for another. Nevertheless, sometimes it was necessary. He always made sure everyone knew up-front that schedules would most likely conflict.

It was rare for him to make more than one trip a day to Tampa. He wondered if he shouldn't take over the business side of running the shuttle and let his brother do the runs a few times so he could experience the stress firsthand.

As he pushed his phone into his pocket, it buzzed again. "Hello, Caroline."

"Uncle Charlie, I forgot to tell you earlier. . .and I couldn't tell you last night because you weren't home when I stopped by to drop off the shuttle and pick up my car. By the way, where were you? You're always there when I come."

Charlie pondered his answer. "Well. . ."

"Okay. I get it. It's none of my business. Forget I asked."

Charlie breathed a sigh of relief. Most of his family wouldn't understand a man's longings for companionship. His whereabouts last night would remain his secret for now.

Carolyn began rattling on again. "Anyway, I neglected to fill up with gas before I dropped the van off. I had planned on doing it this morning."

"I'll get it, don't worry."

"Thanks, I'll talk to you later."

When Charlie started the engine, the gas gauge teetered near empty. Even so, he knew he had enough gas to get to the discount place on the other side of Bradenton. He cut down some side streets to save time and ran into construction. His throat burned. It must have been the orange juice. The stress of his impatience induced a headache that clamped a vise around the center of his head. He'd grab a small bottle of milk after he pumped his gas.

As Charlie pulled into the gas station drive, the shuttle engine died. Thankfully, it coasted just far enough for the gas hose to reach. As he waited for the tank to fill, his eyes drifted to a young man walking in his direction. As he came closer, Charlie waved. "Bill?"

"Mr. Parish?" Bill's handshake was firm.

"Oh my. I haven't seen you in a long time. How you been?"

"Today's been a terrible day. How're you doing?"

"It's been busy for me, even after I turned the company over to Roger."

"I heard you transferred the power. How's he doing?"

"He's as successful as ever. What's got you upset?"

"My Blazer. It gave up the ghost a few hours ago, and I'm stuck here in Bradenton."

"I know a few guys in the auto repair business. Maybe I can give one a call to come help you."

"My dealer is sending a tow truck. Supposedly, they're going to be sending a rental car this afternoon sometime. I gotta get back to Tampa by nightfall for my little girl's Suzuki recital."

"Tampa? Today's your lucky day, Bill. I'm headed up there right now to pick up a load of people. Want a ride?"

"You going to the airport?"

"Yep."

"You bet! I'll call Jan and have her pick me up there. You don't know how much this means to me, Charlie. I owe you."

Charlie waved his hand. "Nah, you don't owe me a thing. You just have to sit there and listen to me try to convince you to change your life around."

"Can't do that, Charlie. Jan already convinced me."

"No kidding?"

"No kidding. She has me going to church and everything. I had to come to the place where I figured out what the important things in life were to me. I had to put God up there at number one. I've felt His peace ever since."

"I wish you could get your claws into Roger and Joyce."

Bill stuffed his hands into his pockets. "I'll do that. I'm coming down here on business again in a couple of weeks. I'd be glad to run that ornery guy down. How's Dan doing?"

Charlie set the gas hose back on the pump. "He hasn't been the same since his girlfriend died. He's out in Hollywood, hoping to land a big part. He takes on a bunch of odd jobs to get by. I wanted him to come help Rog run the citrus business, but he wasn't interested." Charlie checked the change in his pocket then looked back at Bill. "I'm headed in for a milk. Want anything?"

"I'm good."

"I'll be right back out." Charlie strolled to the cooler at the back of the convenience store to get his milk. Just as he raised his hand to the door handle, the dizziness hit him again. A sharp pain in his chest nearly sent him to his knees. He grasped the handle and leaned into the glass door. He could still breathe okay and, after a few minutes, the spell passed.

He eased the door open and allowed the cool air to flow over him. While he stood there slowly inhaling, the clerk hurried down the aisle toward him.

"Mister, it costs money to keep those things cooled. Do you mind shutting the door?"

He nodded at the young man and shut the door. The clerk yanked the milk out of his hand and met him back up in the front of the store. Charlie dropped three dollars on the counter then walked out. He took a few more deep breaths before he opened his door. "You still have your public passenger license from driving the school bus? I could use that hour to relax a bit."

"I do, and I'd be glad to drive. By the way, I called Jan. She thanks you from the bottom of her heart." Bill walked around the van to the driver's side.

Charlie rubbed his chest. "Too much exercise. I'm not used to working out. I'm going to have to take it slower, I guess."

"You're a little pale. Not feeling well?"

"Nah, I'm okay."

"You have to be careful with exercise and not get carried away. Are you sure you're all right?"

Charlie cleared his throat a couple of times then headed for the passenger's seat. "I'm okay."

twelve

The heavy traffic bore Emily along slower than she would have liked. Fortunately, she had allowed enough time for the unexpected. She was glad not to have her SUV because the spot in the parking garage about a block away from Mr. Parish's office barely gave her enough room to park.

The temperature indicator showed the outside temperature was already eighty-four degrees. The motor idled with the air-conditioning set to high while she brushed a bit more color across her cheeks. *You'd be proud of me, Jennifer.* Emily plucked the tube of sunscreen from the inside pocket of her purse and squeezed a dab of lotion on her fingertips to swipe across her cheeks and nose.

When she stepped out of the car, she felt her shoe sink into something soft, then glanced down. *Who would throw his gum out where people walk?* One tissue in the bottom of her purse wasn't enough to get all the gum off her sole. She hobbled around to the front of the car and tried to scrape it off on the cement.

While most of the peppermint glob remained behind, a growing bump under her foot collected pieces of debris from the sidewalk as she headed for Mr. Parish's office. By the time she arrived, her shoe had collected enough remains to glue together a bird's nest.

The hour markers that rested beneath the crystal cover of her Versace watch indicated she had about a minute to get there. She paused long enough to scrape her shoe one more time on the sidewalk then raced up the steps to Mr. Parish's office.

The lemony scent of mahogany met her when she walked through the door. A melodious clock playing "Around the World in Eighty Days" sounded its last note as she closed the door behind her. Emily had made her schedule. "Good morning. Is anyone here?"

A woman elevated by yellow spiked heels and old enough to be her mother, peeked around the corner. "How y'all doin' today? Are you Mrs. Cameron?"

Emily held her hand out to shake the woman's hand. "Yes, I am."

"I'm Clare. Mr. Parish'll be right with you. I'm a little harried right now." Clare pushed a button on her copier that sent out a screech and a moan without any copies. "Please have a seat. Can I get you a bottled water while you're waiting?"

"Yes, thank you."

"Comin' right up."

Emily's eyes followed the stately female as she scurried across the room to a wood-enclosed, apartment-size refrigerator situated on the floor. Emily pretended she didn't hear the cracking as Clare lowered herself to open it. With water in hand, Clare marched with ease across the carpeted floor with not one bobble in her four-inch heels.

"I love your shoes."

"Oh, these old things? They were my sister's before she passed away. All her shoes were like this, crazy and high. We used to trade back and forth. My nephew thinks I'm extreme for trying to navigate in these things, but I've done it my whole life. They say if you're used to wearing heels all the time, you should never try to wear anything else like tennis shoes." She lowered herself into the brown leather chair across from Emily. Their eyes focused on the opening door.

"Mrs. Cameron?"

Emily stood and nodded at the towering man dressed in

blue sweats. "Mr. Parish?"

"Yes, ma'am." His long stride propelled him across the room in a split second. The generous smile and warm hand he offered put her immediately at ease.

"I'm so pleased to meet you, finally."

"I see you've met Aunt Clare." The man accented the last word of every sentence with a high tone.

"She has been delightfully kind to me." Emily threw her a quick smile.

"Well, let's not tarry any longer. I have been chompin' at the bit over this plan you have to save me money. I've checked in with some of the references you've given me, and I can see you possess a bevy of satisfied customers. Come on in." He ruffled all ten fingers through his hair like a dog after fleas. The mass was so black it had a blue cast to it. "Excuse my loungewear. I just got back from the health club."

Emily followed him into his office. "That's okay. I work out, too. You have to work it in whenever you can in a thriving business like the one you operate."

With his head, he motioned toward a chair. "That's right; that's right."

Emily chuckled to herself. They must inject everyone down here with happiness. He hadn't stopped grinning from the time he walked into the room. Her shoe continued to grab on the pile of the new-looking carpet in his office. "I'm so glad it worked out for you to meet with me this morning."

"Me, too; me, too. I tell you it's like pulling teeth sometimes to find a break in my schedule, but Clare helped me work you in." He pulled a chair out for her to sit in as Clare peeked in the room. "Let me know if y'all need anything more."

"Thanks, Aunt Clare." He moved around to his massive chair behind a desk that easily took up a fourth of the room. "I have to apologize ahead of time, Mrs. Cameron. I know your time is valuable, but I have an unavoidable situation taking place. I may have to interrupt our appointment to take a conference call."

"I understand." Emily didn't like to rush through her presentations, but obviously, with a man of his stature and heavy schedule, she had to clinch the deal quickly. She positioned her briefcase on her lap, flipped the latches, and removed the bulging folder. "I know you'll be pleased with the plans and strategies I've suggested for improvement. I've prepared three separate documents for you to peruse at your convenience."

After she had worked through half of her presentation, a startling drone buzzed into the room. "Roger? The company from Mexico is ready for the conference call. Would you like me to ring in Bud Davis from Texas?"

"Yes, thank you, Clare. Thank you. I'll take that call now down the hall in my study." Mr. Parish pushed away from his desk energetically then walked around to take Emily's hand. "I'm so sorry, Mrs. Cameron. I'm so sorry. I'll rush through. I hope you can wait for me."

"I appreciate your working me in this morning. I can wait."

A sweeping motion of his arm opened the room to her. "Please feel free to browse my hall of infamy. That wall over there holds my family portraits, and this wall behind you holds many treasured photos taken of our wonderful company and staff over the years. Again, feel free to browse. Can I get you any coffee, anything to drink?"

Emily stood to her feet. "I'm fine, Mr. Parish. I love to look at photos. I'll be waiting right here for you."

"Thank you, ma'am. Thank you. I'll be back as soon as possible. Please, make yourself at home. Make yourself at home."

As the door closed behind him, a yawn escaped from her

mouth. After positioning her paperwork in sequence on Mr. Parish's desk, Emily rose to peruse the photos. *The wretched shoe*. She pulled it off and turned it over to see a mass of fiber attached to the bottom. Using a scrap of paper she found in her briefcase, she picked at the glob until most of it came off then put her shoe back on.

She moved closer to the far wall and caught sight of a flock of children's photos. A vertical row displayed four separate baseball teams. One team wore blue. The next wore green. The third had black, and the fourth had blue. The consecutive dates on the photos revealed the citrus company sponsored the Southland Indians each year. A close study revealed who the prize player was. Buddy Parish's name was autographed on each picture. His smile stretched as big as Roger Parish's did. *Must be his son.*

Two antique gold frames displayed the beauty of ballet. One held a throng of costumed soldiers in red and blue, marching with guns aimed at some unfortunate mice. The other depicted a multitude of little girls dressed like fairy princesses holding lit Christmas trees. Emily reminisced about Jennifer's childhood and her then hectic schedule in preparation for her role in *The Nutcracker*.

Numerous photos of Roger and his family spread across the remainder of the wall. The array sparked loneliness in Emily's heart for Stan and the way things used to be in her family. Stan played a major role in defining the lives of their children.

Nevertheless, her meeting with Charlie had opened a new page in her life. Scenes materialized that she hadn't expected. New chapters had been inserted. Did he feel as young, alive, and needed again as she did?

Tipping the water bottle to her lips, she moved back across the room. Her eyes strayed to the opposite wall, the wall where corporate dreams come true were displayed. Bold black letters emblazoned across the top of the wall said it all. SOUTHLAND CITRUS COMPANY SUCCESSES.

Aerial views of orange groves from various angles vividly portrayed the massive business Roger and his family had operated. It was easy to see from the photos that members of this family weren't just in business to make money. They cared about people. It was the people who had made it all possible. Adults and children alike peppered the photos of the grove workers. The diversity of employment and age groups boggled her mind.

A framed newspaper article that stretched over two pages of print stood out in the middle of the wall. As she read, she found the details of the process of making juice from the moment the orange plants are grafted into others in the groves to the factory process where the oranges are sorted and made into juice.

Emily couldn't help but allow her mind to drift back again to when she first had Jennifer. At that point, all hope of ever becoming a successful businessperson had vanished. She lived at home, studied for her GED, and worked part-time while her mother babysat. God's amazing grace had forgiven Emily's sins and given her hope for her future. After she received her GED, she applied to and was accepted at Butler University in Indianapolis.

She uncapped her water again and brought it to her lips. The next photo had to be Aunt Clare as a younger woman. She stood in the middle of a grove, holding a bushel basket full of oranges. *Hmm, no heels in this picture.*

Her attention riveted on the next framed newspaper clipping: PARISH FAMILY WORKS IN GROVE ON AWARD DAY. The color photo was set in the groves, and everyone wore orange sweatshirts with the Southland Citrus logo across the front. Under each logo, a name was embroidered. One woman's name was Nancy Belle. Next to her stood a gorgeous man, every bit of whom could be Roger's twin. As she looked closer, she noticed the name on his shirt—Charlie.

Emily's shoulders dropped as the open water bottle slipped out of her limp hand, pouring itself into the plush carpet and onto her shoes. Her gaze froze on the Chamber of Commerce's businessman of the year: Roger Charles Parish, Senior, president of Southland Citrus Company. *Charlie's name is Roger? He was president?*

ও

As long as he sat still, Charlie could forge through the dull ache that worked up from his stomach into his shoulder and into his arm. The inability to breathe right scared him, though. It wasn't that long ago his friend from church had passed on due to some lung disease. He'd had problems breathing at the end. Nevertheless, Charlie knew fear was playing a big part in his anxiety over the pain.

"You okay, Charlie? You look uncomfortable."

"What? Me? Yeah, I'm okay. Nothing a little rest won't clear up." Charlie had been daydreaming about what had transpired over the last few days. Time ticked away slowly when contentment waited at the end of the day. Emily had promised to meet him at the pier to watch the sunset. Impatience prodded at him all day. Compound that with his health issues, and he felt like he would explode. Would she want a sick man?

When they arrived at the airport, Bill pulled up to the cell phone lot. "There she is, patiently waiting for me. Thanks, Charlie. Hey, don't wait around to have that pain checked out. It could be something serious."

"I will. Give your little one a hug for me."

"I'll get in touch with Roger."

Charlie walked around to the driver's side then drove to the shuttle area to wait in his usual parking spot. Not everyone had arrived by the time he pulled in. One of the passengers didn't look too happy.

When Charlie stepped out of the van to greet them all, the man held six tickets up to Charlie's nose. "It's about time someone got here. Do you know how long I've been waiting? These are circus tickets for me, my wife, and my kids. If you don't get us down to Anna Maria in time for us to make it to Sarasota, I'll have your job, *and* you'll pay for these tickets."

Charlie refused to make eye contact, knowing that today's stress had definitely lowered his boiling point. He loaded the luggage, ignoring the burning that seemed to be everywhere. Within a few minutes, six other passengers arrived.

The man with the tickets herded his family on the van first. "I hope you know my family will not give up a seat for anyone. We paid for this shuttle and I expect, at least, to have my own seat."

Charlie pursed his lips and slowly raised his head to the man's eye level. "You've no cause to be angry. We'll work something out."

The two ladies who arrived last had more sunshine in their souls than Florida had in the whole state. They motioned to the only empty seat. One of them assured Charlie. "Don't worry about us. We're small enough to sink into a seat together."

Although he knew he was breaking the rules, Charlie pasted on a smile, leaned over to help secure the two older women in one seat, and then took his own seat, fastening his belt loosely around his body. The trip back to the island proved to be tense, unforgiving, and painful.

As they headed into the downtown area, he ran into another traffic snarl. Two of the children on the shuttle bickered with one another while their father let off a little more steam with Charlie as his target.

When the man began cursing over the traffic, Charlie had had enough. He steered the van to the side of the street, unbuckled his belt, and stood to his feet. He pointed his finger at the man and walked toward him. The next thing Charlie remembered was falling to the floor.

❧

"It's been my pleasure meeting with you, Mrs. Cameron. I'll spread the word that you'll be doing more business in the area. With a little luck, we'll get you started on establishing a strong presence here in Florida."

Emily knew her success had nothing to do with luck. "I appreciate that, Mr. Parish. Hopefully, I'll flourish as well as you have down here."

He stuffed his hands into his pockets. "I have to admit, I owe that to my father. He started with nothing more than a few orange trees and a roadside stand. I was born into the business. I was born into it."

Emily motioned to the wall of newspaper stories. "I see what you mean."

Roger walked over to the wall. "A lot of people think my dad and mom staged this photo with the orange sweatshirts. Not so. My dad loved being in the midst of the workers. He spent most of his time out there getting to know them and picking oranges himself. You rarely found him in a stuffy office."

"I see you have your father's name."

He nodded. "I go by Roger. He goes by Charlie."

If she didn't have confirmation before, she had it now. That was her Charlie. Her neck muscles tightened. "I'm sure he's proud of you."

"Yep, he is; he is."

"Well, thank you, again. I'll see you tomorrow morning so we can go over our projected schedule." Roger stepped ahead of Emily to open the door for her. "I look forward to it."

With contract in hand and a new picture of Charlie Parish in her mind, Emily headed down the stairs. *Charlie Parish, president?* She remembered that father and son both had the same name when she did her research on the company, but it didn't register when she met Charlie. Nothing could have been further from her imagination than to find that she had fallen for someone who had another dimension to his life—one that equaled hers.

She was beginning to see that God truly did have her in the palm of His hand. In spite of her insipid relationship with Him lately, He had blessed her life. *God, I'm so sorry for giving You my leftover time. You are so good to me.*

Emily swung open the door and got blasted with hot temperatures and sirens. Her first sight was the conversion van pulled to the side of the street. She discarded the niceties she might normally have extended to others and pushed her way through the crowd. A pain jabbed her heart when she saw the EMTs carry the recognizable man on a stretcher.

Before she knew it, she had propelled herself to his side. "Charlie? You okay? Charlie?"

He shot her a bashful smile. "Emily. I'm okay. I just passed out. Nothing to worry about."

Emily followed along as Charlie was loaded into the ambulance. She directed her attention to an attendant. "Where are you taking him?"

"Over to Manatee."

Emily turned her attention back to Charlie. "What can I do? Shall I go with you?"

Charlie shook his head and waved to her as the ambulance driver closed the back doors. She followed the driver around to the front of the ambulance. "Shall I notify his son?"

"No, ma'am. He gave us his number. We've contacted the hospital, and they've taken care of it."

Helpless, she watched as a police officer pulled the van into a parking spot and the ambulance headed around the block. She had known Charlie only five days and, already, she felt close enough to become involved. Nevertheless, he let her know he didn't need anything.

Zigzagging across the street and through the slowed traffic, she slipped her jacket off and traipsed into the parking garage to the Toyota. *Calm down, Emily, or you're not even going to get the key in the door.* Heat and exhaust collecting inside the garage from passing vehicles exacerbated her already throbbing temples. Once she was inside, she dropped her briefcase and purse to the floor and jabbed her key into the ignition. Cool air circulated throughout the car.

Why? Streaming tears left gooey mascara clinging to her cheeks. Her purse contents lay scattered on the floor. Pain in her eye sockets stabbed at her until she pressed her fingertips into them and took a few deep breaths.

She didn't even remember driving down the garage drive or opening her window. Nevertheless, her turn signal flashed for five minutes while she waited for someone to let her out onto the street. Eventually, an old Volkswagen bus clunked to a halt, even though its exhaust didn't. Coughing, she waved her thanks, pushed the button to close the window, and pulled out into traffic. At the first stoplight, she pushed the CONTACTS button on her cell and plugged in Hattie's number.

"Hi, y'all. This is Hattie. Leave a message. Thanks."

"Hattie, I need you to pick up your phone. Something's happened." She punched in the number again.

"Hi, y'all. This is Hattie. Leave a message. Thanks."

"Hattie, please call me back immediately. I need to talk to you." Emily snapped her phone shut and laid it on the seat. Before long, she pulled off into a fast-food restaurant about halfway out to the island and headed to the drive-through window. She ordered a diet drink and parked in the lot. Something had to change in her life, and now was as good a time as any.

&

Hattie lifted the whistling ceramic teakettle from the stove as Linda and Emily sat on the lanai, staring out at the Gulf. "Who wants sugar?"

Linda nudged Emily. "You want sugar?"

Emily stirred from her gaze transfixed on the water and yelled in to Hattie. "Yes, two sugars out here, please."

A minute later, the china rattled on the bamboo serving tray as Hattie set it down on the table. "Now, let's talk about today."

Emily reached for a cup and held it out for Hattie. "I never imagined I'd see this happening to Charlie Parish. Then I find out that he is related to Roger. Both men are Roger Charles Parish. Can you believe it?"

Linda waited for Hattie to fill her cup then lifted it from the tray. "How'd you find out?"

Emily bobbed a chamomile tea bag in the steaming water. "At my meeting." She sprinkled a teaspoon of sugar over her tea then squeezed some fresh lemon in. "I saw a photo on the wall in his office. The local Chamber was honoring Charlie and his first wife for their accomplishments. The write-up was framed and hanging on the wall. It was a newspaper clipping. Under his picture were the words, PRESIDENT OF SOUTHLAND CITRUS. I was delighted, surprised, and disappointed, all at the same time."

Linda lifted out her tea bag and squeezed it against a spoon. "That's not what you expected, but that's what you got."

"Don't be disappointed!" said Hattie.

"Now, he's in the hospital."

Hattie stood, then scooted her chair next to Emily. She clasped her arms around Emily's shoulders. "Don't you think this is a God-given opportunity to show your concern?"

Emily swiveled. "I hear my phone buzzing on the dining room table."

Hattie beat her to her feet. "Got it." Hattie handed her the phone. "It's Mr. Parish—Roger Parish."

Emily set her teacup on the table and took the phone from Hattie. "Mr. Parish?"

"Yes, this is Roger Parish calling. Is this Mrs. Cameron?"

Emily opted to play as if she didn't know anything. "Thank you for calling so soon, Mr. Parish. Do you need more information?"

"Business wise, everything is fine. I just got a phone call from a rep at the hospital. Dad's been rushed there by ambulance. He's apparently had some heart problems. I won't make our meeting to lay out our strategy tomorrow."

Emily sprang up out of the chair. "A heart attack? Is he okay?"

"I don't know yet. I'm here at the emergency room at the hospital. We're still waiting for his doctor to come in; we're still waiting."

Emily felt the blood drain from her face as she paced back and forth between the living room and the lanai. "Please keep me informed."

"I'll be calling you."

She held the phone out to Hattie and Linda. "Heart attack."

thirteen

Emily fell silent as she lowered herself to the couch. "No, not Charlie."

Linda and Hattie joined her.

"Someone please check to see if they picked up the rental car yet."

Emily stared vacantly as Hattie rushed down to the front of the condo and back again. "It's still there."

Emily shot from the couch. "Let's go. I can't just sit here and wonder."

Linda nodded. "We'll take you."

"I'm ready. Thanks for helping, you two. I don't know what I'd do without you."

Linda handed Emily her purse and maneuvered her out the door. "Go on down to the car. I'll lock everything up and be right down."

Hattie raced ahead, slipped in behind the wheel, pulled down the visor, and pinched her cheeks. "Okay, which way are we going?"

Emily fiddled with her lipstick. "Manatee. It's the hospital you pass on the way in from the airport."

Hattie turned the key in the ignition as Linda scrambled into the car. Emily pondered her situation. While this had all the earmarks of tragedy, she hoped for the best. Gradually, she was realizing Charlie Parish was meant to be in her life for more than five days.

❧

"There it is. I see the sign." Hattie careened around the corner and turned in the circular drive to the entrance. "Will this be okay, or do you want to go to the emergency room?"

Emily weighed the appropriateness of showing up in the emergency room where Charlie's family probably waited with him. "I believe we're doing it the right way. Just let me off up here."

Hattie glanced off to her left. "I think we'll be in that parking area. We'll watch for you to come back out. Good luck, honey."

The drifting aroma of coffee met Emily when she entered the hospital lobby. Her nose followed the scent to a steaming cup sitting in front of the receptionist. She glanced around for a familiar face then laughed at herself. She didn't know anyone here except for Charlie and Roger. The woman behind the desk smiled as Emily walked closer. "Can you tell me where to find a patient named Charlie Parish?"

After rummaging through some papers, the woman pointed to the elevator. "It looks as though he's just been transferred." She scribbled on a sticky note. "Here's his room number."

The fragrance of the busy lobby soon gave way to the sterile aroma of gauze and alcohol. As Emily squeezed into the elevator, she rehearsed the greeting she would offer Charlie. By the time she had stepped off onto his floor, she had reconsidered. What if Charlie was only passing time when he had invited her to dinner? Was that common for him? She depressed the button to head back downstairs to the lobby. Then she called to mind how he had taken her hand in his.

Emily gradually drifted to his room. She paused outside the door, planted her feet firmly, and took a deep breath. While she didn't want to intrude on the conversation that took place inside the room, the two voices were unmistakable: Charlie and Roger Parish. She tapped her knuckles on the door and waited.

The moment the invitation was given, she entered the

room. Roger rose to his feet. In spite of the sunlight streaming through the windows on the other side of the bed, she noticed Charlie's beaming smile. "Emily." He waved his hand for her to come closer.

With a question on his face, Roger gripped her hand then produced a chair for her.

"Thanks, Mr. Parish, but I'll stand."

"Mrs. Cameron, I didn't expect you to come all this way to visit my father. It sounds like you two already know each other."

Charlie's jaw dropped. "How do you know Emily?"

"I had a meeting with her in my office earlier today. Later I had to call her and tell her I wouldn't be meeting with her tomorrow because of your incident. That's probably why she's here now."

Charlie shifted his face from Roger to Emily and gave a half smile. "Emily, is this the business appointment you told me you had today?"

"Yes, Charlie, but I had no idea this was your son until I noticed your photograph on the wall in his office." She glanced to Roger, now hovering over her.

"Dad, Mrs. Cameron has a thriving business in Indianapolis. Many consider her to be tops in her field. You must have taken her to the island in your shuttle."

Emily shifted her stance. "Your father never asked what I did for a living, and I never told him." She cast a glance to Charlie and shrugged. "I hope you feel better soon, Charlie. If there's anything I can do, please let me know."

Nothing else came to her mind to say. Roger was Charlie's son. If he had any insight at all, and she believed he did, he may have concluded Emily had a soft spot in her heart for his father.

Charlie pushed the button to raise the head of his bed

higher. "I won't be here long. They can't find any serious reason for my episode. I'm told a little rest, a good diet, and exercise ought to get me back in gear."

"Now, Dad, you probably won't be doing any exercising for a while. Joyce and I were thinking you should pack some things and come stay with us for a spell."

Emily couldn't mistake the cry for help in Charlie's eye. She wanted to stay with him for a while, to take his hand and confirm her support. Nevertheless, he had to make that call, if he wanted to. "I can't stay for long. I just wanted to check on things. Let me know where you'll be staying, Charlie." She reached to shake Roger's hand. "Mr. Parish, call me when you'd like to meet again."

Roger showed her to the door. "Thank you for coming. That means a lot to us. I'll keep in touch."

Emily turned one last time and caught Charlie's smile and wave. She avoided the slow elevator, walked down the steps past the receptionist's desk, and pushed her way out the front door. As she scanned the parking lot, Hattie drove up the circle.

As soon as Emily set foot in the car, she let out a moan. "I'm glad that's over."

Hattie took her foot off the brake and shifted the gear to park. "You're glad what's over?"

"The charade. I believe Charlie would have liked me, no matter who I was. Roger was up there visiting. Of course, our business relationship was revealed. Charlie didn't seem upset when he discovered I have a successful business in Indiana."

"Is he okay?" said Linda.

Exhaustion had conquered Emily, and so had her love for Charlie. "No heart problems. That's all I know. Let's get out to the beach. I need to process all this and wait to see if he ever calls me again."

❧

The beeping heart monitor from the room to the right of his, the alarms from the room on his left, and the midnight check of his vitals had kept Charlie from experiencing a sound sleep the night before. All night he thought about contacting Emily, but he thought she might not want to talk to him now.

He ran his fingers around the neckline of his hospital gown to find the opening in the back then loosened the cord, which was tied too tightly around his neck. Roger had insisted that he spend the night for observation. *Time to get out of here.*

Ruminating on the information that had exploded yesterday had made his quest for Emily's attentions all the more clear now. He needed to talk to her. *Wow. Who could have orchestrated this, other than You, Lord? Emily and I were made for each other.*

Charlie shoved the covers to the end of his bed and swung his legs over the edge just as Doctor Andresi popped into the room. "How are we doing today, Mr. Parish?" The depth of the doctor's Indian accent kept Charlie in the dark most of the time as to what he actually said. Doctor Andresi lifted Charlie's chart from the foot of the bed.

"I'm ready to get out of here."

The doctor raised his brows, walked closer, and gripped Charlie's shoulder. "Are we having pain?"

Charlie wrinkled his forehead and stared at him for a moment. "No, no pain. Listen, Doc, you've got to help me stay on my own. My son wants to whisk me away from my home and keep me under lock and key at his house."

Doctor Andresi chuckled. "That's normal for the children to do. However, you're too young and too well for that, Mr. Parish. I'll see what I can do. I see, by your chart, your vitals are good. I hope they're just as good next time we see each other."

"There won't be a next time. I started changing my lifestyle yesterday, just before I passed out."

"Good. Good." Using his stethoscope, the doctor listened to the center of Charlie's chest, then his back. "Mr. Parish, I must say, you are fine. Sometimes, indigestion or acid reflux can charade as heart problems. I have people all the time swear that they are having a heart attack. I reassure them they're only experiencing stomach acid. I'll have my associate work with you on diet and an exercise plan. I don't want to see you back here again, for any reason. Your heart is okay for a man your age."

"And you'll clear things with my son?"

He fiddled with his chin as he chuckled from his throat. "Yes. Don't worry. When I am finished with your son, he will know you are in charge, as they say. You will be free to go as soon as all the paperwork is finished. Do you have someone to take you home?"

"I'll find someone."

The doctor left, and Charlie poked at the food sitting on his table. After two bites of something that looked like real eggs, he covered it back up and jotted some names down on his napkin. Emily's name was at the top of the list. Thoughts of their last dinner together had him convinced she'd be the one to call.

A light rap sounded on his open door. "Hey, partner."

Charlie motioned. "Ted, come in. Have a seat. Well, how do I look?"

Ted pulled a plastic chair over to the bed. "You look pretty pathetic, I have to say. How'd you end up here?"

"Who called you?"

"Roger. He allowed you one phone call, so to speak. I have to say, he sounded tremendously worried."

"Ted, Roger just loves to hover over me and think he's in charge. He knows he can't keep me prisoner against my will." Charlie rang the buzzer for the nurse to come. "As soon as I get the okay, I want you to take me home, Ted."

Ted stood to his feet. "So nothing's wrong?"

"I only had indigestion. Doctor Andresi said I could go home, to my own home, if someone could take me. Come on, Ted. You can't let me be taken captive by my ambitious son."

Ted rolled his shirtsleeve back to see his watch. "Okay, what time can you leave?"

"I need to wait until one of the nurses finishes her paperwork. Then I'm free."

"What about your lady friend? Anything going on there?"

"You won't believe this." Charlie pushed himself up in the bed. "She owns her own consulting business. Ted, she had a meeting with my son yesterday. Roger called her to cancel their next appointment because of me. Of course, he didn't know she knew me. She came up here to visit me. Boy, was Roger surprised. I was surprised."

Ted chuckled. "Amazing how God brings a plan together in a way we don't expect. Am I reading love between the lines?"

Charlie felt the color leave his face. "Come back around one o'clock, Ted. I should be ready to go by then."

Ted flashed a smile and smacked him on the arm. "I'll be back, buddy. We'll escape and travel to your abode on the beach."

Within the hour, a nurse came in and handed Charlie his paperwork. "There you go. Sorry I took so long. According to Doctor Andresi, you can do whatever you want."

"Go home?"

"Feel free. Do you have clothes?"

Charlie responded with a nod.

"Well, I'll leave you to it then." As she headed out, Roger walked around the corner.

"Hey, Dad." Roger gave Charlie a pat on the back. "Sounds like you can go now."

"Morning, Roger. Before you say anything else, I'm not

going home with you."

"It's for your own good. You can't go back to the beach in this condition."

"Roger, I'd love to come and see the kids, but Doctor Andresi suggested I go to my own home. He said I'm in good enough shape to do that. All I need to do is follow my diet and exercise. I plan to do just that."

"Joyce cleaned out her hobby room just for you. It's on the lower floor and you won't have to go up and down stairs like you do out at the beach."

"Going up and down stairs will be good for me, son. That's what I'm going to do. I love you and Joyce, but I haven't kicked the bucket yet. I still have a lot of years remaining in these old bones and I'm not going to throw them away. Doc said I only have indigestion. Too many doughnuts. Trust me, I've learned my lesson. And, Rog, do you have my phone?"

Roger laid the cell phone on the accessory table. "Now I know where I get my independent spirit, Dad. I wouldn't want to leave my home either, if I didn't have to. Can I drive you?"

"I've already enlisted Ted. If it offers any comfort to you, I'm sure he'll hover over me worse than you would. Can the kids come out to the beach next week? I'll rent a sailboat and take them out in the Gulf."

"They'd love that. I'm sure Joyce will want to go along."

Charlie threw his arms around Roger as they slapped each other on the back. Charlie couldn't wait to see Emily. She had improved his outlook on life by 200 percent, at least. The anticipation of seeing her seemed almost as good as being with her.

Now that they had discovered one another's lot in life, they had even more in common. He had fallen in love and only had until the end of the week to tell her. If she reciprocated, he'd be the winner. He didn't want to consider the other option.

fourteen

"Come on, don't be so reluctant." Hattie tugged on Emily's arm, leading her out closer to the water.

Emily stopped to slip her sandals off her feet then threw them on her towel. "I'd love to go in, but what if Charlie calls? I'll have to spend an hour getting cleaned up and ready to see him."

"Emily, give me a break," said Linda. "Relax. This is Florida. Enjoy the sand and surf."

Hattie and Linda coaxed her as far as the water's edge. Emily relaxed as the cool surf lapped up over the top of her bare feet. Eventually, she edged out knee-deep. Finally, she collapsed into the surf.

"How's it feel, girl?" said Hattie.

"It feels like I should have jumped in here days ago. Why'd you insist I do it today?"

Hattie dropped into the water next to her. "You needed to have some fun. This romance with Charlie has you all tied up in knots."

"I'm not tied up in knots. I'm simply flustered. I'm worried about what Stan would have thought. And"—she frowned— "I'm afraid I'm acting like a fool." Emily left the water and grabbed a beach towel. "I can't decide whether to nix my feelings or jump in full speed ahead."

Linda followed. "Neither Roger Parish nor Charlie seem to have a problem with you, right?"

"You're right and, although I hope I'm not jumping to conclusions, I've decided to call my office today to see if

Carson will continue to fill in for another week. Then I'll see if I can find another condo and contact the airlines to reschedule my flight. I'm not heading out until a week from Sunday."

"Emily! That's more like it!" said Hattie. "We're your friends, and if your friends can't talk to you, then who can? We've thought all along this man had something special to offer you, remember?"

Emily brushed the towel against her legs then spread it out on the sand. "The fact remains, neither one of us is who we thought the other was."

Hattie spread her towel next to Emily. "Honey, I've known you for over forty years and I think I have a handle on what you need. This man is what you need. I wasn't so sure when I first heard that you wanted virtually to be unknown out here. Maybe you were right. Now, at least, you know he's not some pauper after you for your money."

Hattie and Emily dropped to their towels. Linda sat on the other side of Emily. "Look at the big picture. You're in love with the gentleman. I've worked alongside you and Stan. You've been faithful to him—even for the year he's been gone. Now, it seems you've found room in your heart for Charlie. You have a new man who's come on the scene. One of you has to have the courage to admit your attraction to the other."

Emily closed her eyes and nodded. "Yes, I have to say that's true. Do you think Stan would mind?"

Linda threw her arm over Emily's shoulder. "Didn't you tell me Stan and you had a talk about that very thing a few years back? Your happiness was paramount to Stan, as was his to you.

"I know that's what he said, but I'm having a difficult time moving past that."

Hattie bumped up against Emily. "Do you want to?"

Using her knuckle, Emily caught a tear rolling down her cheek. "I think I do."

"Then what are you waiting for, girl? Why aren't you up there in that hospital room right now, visiting the man?"

"I called the hospital before we came to the beach. He was dismissed today."

"That's a good thing, Emily. That means he's better," said Hattie.

Emily looked at Hattie, then at Linda, and shrugged her shoulders. "I don't where he lives."

"Can't you call him?" asked Linda.

"I'm not sure I want to do that. I think I just want to see him in person and talk."

"Oh, you want to surprise him? Hmm. . . There are ways to find out where he lives," said Hattie. "Now that you know Roger, won't he tell you?"

"I'm not going to cloud my business relationship with Roger. I believe that would be inappropriate. Maybe Charlie's address is in the phone book."

"Maybe it is," said Linda.

Hattie pulled her towel with her as she stood. "Well, let's run up and check it. We have to start somewhere."

Emily minced across the hot sand, following after her friends. "Do you think this is okay? I don't want to overpower him."

"Maybe he's in the same predicament you are. Maybe he doesn't know his own heart right now," said Hattie.

"It's not that I don't know my own heart." By the time Emily reached the top of the stairs, Hattie had already found Charlie Parish's address. "Here is it, Em. Change your clothes. Fix yourself up. We're going for a walk."

"Not until I call Jennifer." Emily disappeared into her room and pushed her speed dial for Jennifer.

"Hi, Mom. What's up?"

"Jennifer, you're not going to believe this."

❧

Ted nudged Charlie's front door shut with his foot then set the last box of groceries on the floor. "There you go, my friend."

Charlie lifted out two cartons of milk, a box of oatmeal, and two see-through containers holding what looked like grass. "I can't thank you enough, Ted. I feel like I've just received a degree in nutrition."

Ted sank the drain into the sink, turned on the cold water, and emptied in the sack of green beans. "You sure did take the long way around the barn to get to the house, Charlie."

Charlie set six huge tomatoes on the counter next to the sink. "What do you mean by that?"

Ted rustled the beans around in the sink then drained out the water. "If you wanted me to go grocery shopping for you and carry the stuff up the steps, why didn't you just tell me instead of going and having a fake heart attack?"

Charlie laughed and slapped Ted across the back. "You're a good friend, Ted. Next time, I'll be more direct."

"You really going to try to eat fruit—including tomatoes?"

Charlie whipped a paper off the counter and held it in front of Ted's face. "You see what the good doctor wrote for me? Actually, it was the dietician at the hospital. She looked like an army sergeant when she sat across the table from me and told me to follow this or else."

"Ha! Or else what?"

Charlie knocked both ends loose on one of the boxes and stuck the flattened cardboard between the counter and his fridge. "Or else, I'll have to consume mass quantities of antacids and live my life out in pain."

"Whew, that bad, huh?"

"I should have been working out with you long before this.

Look at you. You're the picture of health, just like Emily."

"Speaking of Emily, did you talk to her yet?"

"Nah, I haven't had a chance. Right now, I just need to kick back for a few hours. Grab a piece of fruit and join me on the lanai." Charlie picked up a banana and an apple and preceded Ted out the sliding doors that faced the Gulf.

"Sounds to me like you're making excuses." Ted moved the door halfway across the runner. "Smells better out here than that hospital, eh, Charlie?" He dug his fingernail into the thick orange rind and dropped the peelings on the table.

Charlie peeled back the skin on the banana. "You know, I'd rather be here than any hospital on this earth. Even if I have to skip cake and cookies while I exercise for a while, I'm just glad to be alive and right back here in my own home."

Ted poked his thumb in the middle of the orange, peeled a section, and before stuffing it into his mouth, said, "Roger try to change your mind?"

"Nope. Once I told him I was coming home, he relented." For several minutes Charlie stared out at the rolling waves. Sometimes he wanted to turn time back and relive Roger's and Dan's younger days. The boys had grown up far too quickly and had been on their own before he knew it.

After downing the last section of orange, Ted motioned out to the surf. "It's peaceful out there, Charlie. The constancy of the rolling waves pacifies us. And the peace we have knowing our lives are wrapped up in what God has planned for us—it's amazing."

"Yeah, and the good Lord had His hand on me when my body started to fall apart."

Ted looked him in the eye. "Do you remember the day you asked Him to take over your life?"

Charlie stared back. "Yep, I do."

"I remember that day in my life, too. I sat on the beach in

the sun when two strangers came up and told me how to pray. The point I'm getting at is you and I both willingly gave our hearts and lives over to Jesus."

"Yes, we did, Ted. I don't think you're at your point yet though. What is it you want to say?"

Ted sat back and looked back out over the surf. "It's so easy to get caught up in game playing."

Charlie straightened in his chair. "Yep, I know."

Ted looked over at Charlie. "I'm talking about the woman you've fallen in love with."

He stared straight ahead. "I'm not so sure there's any chance."

"How do you know?"

Apple in hand, Charlie stood and leaned on the rail. "We don't have any time left. Wednesday's almost gone. She'll go home Sunday. That will be the end of it."

"Take a chance. Anyone who can motivate you to exercise has got to be someone special."

"I don't have the guts to do it now. Do you know how embarrassing it is at our age to take some of those steps? Anyway, I don't know if I can do that to Nancy."

Ted stood and leaned his back on the rail. "Nancy hasn't been here for a couple years. I know she loved you, but she's gone, Charlie. You have to come to grips with that. You may not have the guts *now*. It'll come. At least take the first step with Emily. The week's almost gone."

Charlie dug out some apple seeds with his finger and let them drop to the floor. "Can't do that with a woman around."

Ted eyed Charlie. "Are you just looking for excuses not to call her?"

"I'm not very good at this. Do you know what it's like to date after all those years of being happily married? I hate starting over again." Charlie didn't want Ted to think he was weak, but he truly didn't know how to respond. Nor did he have a clue as to where to continue with Emily.

"I've had the same problem dating, but you've never found someone as special as Emily Cameron, right? I think whatever you have to do to get to know her, do it."

Ted's words chunked Charlie right in the heart. Emily's attentions *were* worth pursuing. "I want to do that. But how do I start, and what do I say? I'm at her mercy. She has my cell number, but I don't have hers."

"Didn't you say she called you once? You can get her number from your incoming calls on your phone."

"I had forgotten that."

"Time is of the essence, my friend. We dare not take a chance with time."

"I'll be right back. My phone's in on the counter."

❧

"Mom, I was just thinking about you."

"Oh Jennifer. I'm glad."

"Do I need to come down there?"

"No, honey, it's nothing like that. I just wanted to run something by you."

"Okay. . ."

"It's Mr. Parish. I think our relationship may develop into something more than friendship."

"Mom, no. It's too soon. You don't even know him. What's happened?"

"We've talked, we've shared, and we've connected somehow. I can't explain it."

"Have you talked to Jared? I think you need to call him before you do anything foolish."

"I can't explain my feelings or my thoughts to anyone right now. I just thought I'd let you know, since you had met him. Don't worry. I won't do anything stupid."

"Mom, I'm coming back."

"Wait until I call you again. I'm staying another week down here. We'll leave it at that, okay? There's no sense in your flying down here for no reason."

"Another week? Okay, Mom. Try to get some rest, and don't rush into anything. I'm home the rest of the week. Call me if you need to talk about anything, promise?"

"I will, Jen. Don't worry. I'm fine."

Emily set her phone on the dresser then headed for the shower. The whole matter had her shaken up, and now she had Jennifer on edge. *I never should have called her.* She turned the hot water faucet a little bit further to the left and switched the showerhead to pulsate. The rivulets of water punched into her tense shoulders. It would be ridiculous for her to walk to the beach in front of Charlie's house. What would he think?

A knock on the door gradually became more insistent. "Em? Come on, girl, we have to do this *today*."

Emily closed her eyes under the steamy water. She could stay forever in the penetrating warmth. "Almost done."

"Do you want me to lay out an outfit?"

"No, you stay out of my clothes. I'll take care of it, Hattie. Please, be patient." Emily rubbed the net scrubber over the bar of soap then spread the suds over her body. She rinsed quickly. There was no point resisting when Hattie and Linda had their minds made up. Before long, she emerged to hear them chatting in the hallway. "Don't even say anything. I need to fix my face and hair."

Hattie's gold leather sandals clicked on the ceramic floor. "Okay, honey. We'll be on the lanai."

Emily tousled the towel through her hair as she took stock of the clothes hanging in the closet. She didn't think twice. The real Emily Cameron was about to emerge, stand out in front of Charlie's house on the beach, and enjoy every minute of it.

The jersey cropped pants with the matching jacket would wick the humidity from her skin and look attractive, along with the gray shell. She slipped on leather sandals to match then walked out to meet the other girls. "I'm as ready as I'll ever be. Let's get this over with."

"Don't be so begrudging," said Linda. "This could be the best decision of your life."

Emily threw her hands in the air. "Or the worst. He may get turned off by my insistence."

Hattie poked her finger against Emily's arm. "Emily Rene Cameron, put on your happy face because I have a feeling today is going to be a new beginning for you. Let's go. We'll take the trolley a ways past the old Rich's Beach Drugs building, then we'll walk the rest of the way."

"Wait. I have two questions. What do you mean by *we*, and how do you know where to go?"

Linda walked up behind Emily. "You don't want to go alone, do you?" Linda looked at Hattie then turned back to Emily. "Okay, I hate to admit to it"—she blushed—"but we looked up his address last night. I've got it written right here." Linda handed her a pink sticky note. "We'll go partway then you can go it alone, okay?"

Emily wheezed out a sigh. "I'm losing my courage." She pushed out the door and started down the steps. Hattie and Linda followed down behind her. A pang worked its way into her heart.

Hattie and Linda flanked each side of Emily. It gave her the feeling if she hadn't come willingly, they would have dragged her. Before long, they boarded the trolley and rode as far as the shopping area where the drugstore used to be.

"Come on, let's get off here," said Hattie. She looped her arm through Emily's.

"Are we walking to the beach from here?" asked Emily. "I

thought we'd have to go farther to find his house."

"You're right." Hattie shot a glance to Linda.

"It's not that far," said Linda. "I have another confession. Hattie and I rode down here yesterday while you had your meeting with Roger Parish. We heard there was a little shop around the corner that had unique jewelry."

Emily dabbed the perspiration from her forehead as the three of them made their way around Gulf Drive North. "And. . . ?"

They swerved off onto a side street and continued to walk. "And we walked to see where his house was. So, don't worry. We're almost there." Hattie pointed straight ahead.

Emily gaped at the house then quickly turned around. "I don't think I can do this."

Linda caught her by her jacket sleeve. "Sure, you can. You just walk up the steps by that beautiful magnolia and knock on the door."

"I'd go by the beach way if I were her. Wouldn't that be more romantic?" Hattie nudged Linda with her elbow.

Submerged in a pool of skepticism, Emily threw up her hands. "Can you two listen to yourselves? This is my life here. I can't take this lightly. I'm not some teenage girl ogling after her teenage lover. I'm a mature woman. He's a mature man. Can you imagine what he would think if I carried on the way you two seem to think I should? I'm mortified."

"Whoowee, it sure is getting hot out here," said Hattie. "I could go for a cold diet drink."

Linda shrugged her shoulders and followed Hattie down the street, leaving Emily to her own means. Emily stood silent. *Time to find out what you're made of, Emily Cameron. It's time to lay it all out on the table.*

The public access to the beach was only a short distance away. Emily opted for Hattie's method of doing things. She would feel much more comfortable walking past Charlie's house once or twice before she actually made her cold call.

The scorching sand flipped into her sandals with each step, but she made a beeline for the water's edge. She slipped the sandals off and walked in ankle deep into the surf. The water cooled her and seemed to steady her trembling hands. Doubts crept in as she walked back down the beach toward the house they all had identified as *the* house. She sucked in one breath as she stood directly in front of Charlie Parish's home. *What now?*

fifteen

As Charlie poked the glass into the fresh water well of the refrigerator for his third drink, he pondered contacting Emily. The very thought brought on anxiety. He pivoted to Ted.

"Do I look okay?"

"Yeah."

"I think I'm all right. My heart seems to be working okay, now. I felt like the beat started flopping around."

"It's a false alarm, Charlie. You just need to follow through on what we just talked about and I assure you, things will start to improve rapidly. Your nerves are getting the best of you."

Charlie leaned back against the counter. "Let me ask you a question, Ted. In your experience. . ."

"I have no experience. You know that. Just get the phone and make the call. You'll be glad you did."

"Okay, let's go back out on the lanai. I need the gulls to give me some background music if I intend to woo Emily."

Charlie closed the lanai door behind Ted then poked Emily's number into his cell. After two rings, she answered.

"Emily Cameron."

He took a deep breath and lowered into the chair. There was no pretending that he didn't have feelings for her. "Emily, this is—"

"Charlie! I thought the number looked familiar. Are you feeling better?"

"I will be in a few minutes."

"Why's that?"

Charlie glanced to see Ted prodding him on with his nod. "I have to talk to you, but I'd rather do so in person. Could we meet somewhere?"

"I'd like that. Would you like to meet right now?"

"Now? You tell me where, and I'll be there."

"How about right out in front of your place?"

"What do you mean?"

"Can you see me at the water's edge?"

Charlie's attention shot out to the beach. He stood to focus on the woman out near the water. "Is that you waving?"

"It's me."

"How'd you end up out there?"

Emily started walking toward the house. "It's a long story. Let's just say I have ambitious friends, and they helped me to see I needed to talk to you face-to-face."

"Can you come around to the front of the house? I'll meet you there."

"I saw the steps out there leading up to your deck."

"I'll meet you at the bottom of those stairs."

"Okay, Charlie. It's a date."

Charlie flipped his phone shut then hurried through the house to the front door. By the time he stepped out on the deck, Emily was at the foot of the steps. "May I invite you to join me, Mrs. Cameron?"

She stepped on the first step and peered up at him. "Is it proper?"

"It's proper. We have a chaperone. My lifelong friend is here trying to help me sort through all the fruits and vegetables that fill my kitchen."

"Oh, doctor's orders?"

A flush of anticipation warmed him as she walked up the steps, and he walked down. At the same time, Ted walked out the door. Charlie shouted back at him. "Don't go anywhere,

Ted. I'm entertaining a lady, and she won't be caught here alone with me."

&

Hardly noticing her feet were carrying her up the stairs to stand face-to-face with the man who had stolen her heart, Emily fastened her eyes on Charlie Parish.

Ted gave a nod to Emily. "Mrs. Cameron. I've heard so much about you."

Charlie motioned to Ted. "Emily, this is my friend, Ted. Ted, meet Emily."

Emily extended her hand. "My pleasure."

Charlie spilled his words out like water dancing on hot coals. "Ted was the cook on the boat Sunday. The boat's mine. I'm sorry I didn't tell you then."

She raised her brows. "The funny thing is, I know why you didn't."

"You do?"

"If you're like me, you were sick and tired of feeling like you were a commodity of which everyone wanted a part. Being loved and wanted for who you are is a priceless jewel people like you and I don't find very often. I think deep down inside, I knew it didn't belong to your friend." She motioned to a chair at the table. "May I sit down?"

Charlie bounced a chair from across the deck and invited her to sit in it. "Here you go. This one's been covered from the elements, if you know what I mean."

"I have shopping of my own to do, Charlie," said Ted. "I think I'm going to bow out of here for now. Call me if you need anything."

"Wait, Ted." Charlie's eyes met Emily's. "Are you all right with us being alone here?"

"We're outside, Charlie. I think I can trust you out here where everyone can see us." She batted one eye.

Ted headed for the stairs. "I guess that's my cue. Mrs. Cameron, the pleasure has been all mine."

"Thank you, Ted. Please, call me Emily." She stalled for something to say but didn't have to wait long. Charlie pulled another chair up facing her then he sat down, a smile stretching between his dimples.

He held out an open hand. As she settled hers into his, the same meaningful confirmation, which came on the day when Charlie had helped her into his van at the airport, bore witness to her. Emily allowed the enjoyment to fill her. "I came to apologize to you. Whether or not I felt I had good reason, I was wrong not to be myself." She lifted her eyes to meet his. "I just wanted to see how people would respond to me if I didn't appear to be a corporate leader."

Charlie inched his chair closer to Emily's. His hand tightened around hers. "I'm the one who needs to be forgiven. Even though a good deal of people know me out here on the beach, I've tried to change the way I'm viewed since I turned my citrus company over to Roger. I'm the one who needs your forgiveness."

Emily's words stuck in her throat. She had visions of what she wanted to say, the desire was there to say it, but nothing came. His eyes penetrated hers as she continued to gaze into them. Then she felt him take her other hand. She choked back a sob as he raised her hands to his lips. As he let them graze the back of each hand, she noticed the tears that stopped just short of falling out through those beautiful long lashes of his.

Only whispers left her lips. "Charlie?"

"I know it's only been days since we met. They've been so full. The moment you walked into my life something about you drew me into a different realm. I think I love you, Emily. Isn't that crazy? Me falling in love at my age? So quickly. Maybe it's infatuation. I don't know what it is, but I know I want you to stay in my life. I don't want you to disappear when the plane flies out of Tampa on Sunday. I don't think I could bear it." He kissed her hands again.

"I know." Emily swallowed air while she desperately tried to breathe it in. "I canceled Sunday."

"You did?"

"I know what you're saying. I feel like we're both reading the same page. I sweep into town, and you sweep me off my feet. What are we going to do now? I have a business to run in Indiana."

In a moment's time, Charlie pulled her to her feet and into his arms. The comfort of his touch settled her. Her head nestled into the crook between his neck and his shoulder as she moved her arms around his back. Then she heard Hattie's voice.

"Emily, is that you?"

Emily broke from his embrace and motioned to Hattie and Linda. "Girls, you remember Charlie."

Charlie took Hattie's hand in a brief shake, then Linda's. "Can I get you all some iced tea or lemonade?"

The girls huddled briefly, then Emily turned to face him. "We're going back to our house so you can rest for a while, Charlie. You know where it is. If you feel up to it later, please join us." Emily couldn't mistake the look of love in Charlie's eyes.

"I may take you up on that. Shall I call you first?"

"Yes, please do. You have my cell number."

꙳

Charlie eased the door partway closed. He watched his new love chatter away with her friends as they walked down the street. Thank God he had involved himself in the shuttle business. *Oh no. The shuttle.* He grabbed the cell phone and dialed Caroline's number.

"Hi, Uncle Charlie. How're you doing?"

"Caroline, I forgot about my run this morning."

"I have it covered. Roger called me."

Charlie switched the phone to his other ear. "When did he do that?"

"Yesterday he called me to come get your stranded passengers, and I got there within ten minutes. Boy, was that guy going to the circus with his kids mad. Whooee, I don't want another experience like that one. He could hardly wait until the EMT guys got you off the van so I could take off."

"He wasn't crying over my dilemma then?"

"He could have cared less, Uncle Charlie, but your family is a different story. Roger is worried about you being out there all alone. Wouldn't you have a more comfortable time of it in here with the family?"

Charlie strolled back out on the deck and fixed his gaze on the three women in the distance. "Don't let it bother you. Did Roger tell you what was wrong when he called?"

"No, he called me when they rushed you to the hospital, and then let me know when you went home. I figured I'd have this morning's run."

"I only had indigestion. It was nothing serious. Ted and I bought nearly every vegetable known to man, thanks to my dietician. She has suggested for the time being that I stay away from citrus, but I can eat other fruits as long as they don't bother me. I'm changing my diet, my exercise plan, my whole life."

"We'll see how long that lasts."

"You'll be surprised at my tenacity. Do you want me to take the run tomorrow?"

"Roger asked me if I could do it. I have time between classes. I'll be out to the beach today to pick up the shuttle. I can do it the rest of the week, Uncle Charlie. Why don't you take care of any personal belongings in there, and I'll just keep the van at Mom and Dad's until next week?"

Charlie liked her plan. While he felt well enough to do the runs to Tampa, he welcomed the free time to spend with Emily. He had settled with the fact he didn't like being alone anymore. He resolved there wouldn't be many more days like it. He thought about all the opportunities God had brought his way for companionship. None of them had ever gelled until he met Emily.

Charlie formulated a plan. He could spend some of his time in Indiana. Depending on where Emily was in her business, she could spend some of the time in Florida. He let out a sigh. It would take a miracle for him to talk the plan out with Emily tonight. They had a week. Was that enough time for God to work a miracle?

ঞ

"I saw that look in your eyes when Mr. Right had you captured in his arms up there on the veranda." Hattie plopped down on the bench at the trolley stop under the MCAT sign.

Emily dropped next to her. "It wasn't planned, Hattie. It just happened."

"Did we tell you, or did we tell you?" Linda smiled.

A flood of exhaust preceded the screeching wheels. Emily floated into the trolley. "Come on, slowpokes. I need to get back to the house and figure this all out." Emily walked to the open-air section at the back of the trolley.

Hattie sat opposite her. "Honey, you're radiant. What's to figure out? Your face says it all."

Linda crawled across Emily, sat next to the window, and took a small-size book out of her purse. "So, what's on the agenda for tonight?"

"I'm not sure. I know Charlie said he wanted to come to our place, but I don't know if he'll have enough energy to do it. Going through what he did yesterday had to be exhausting. I'm thinking of calling him and ask if he would prefer me going to his house."

"That's a first for you. You going alone?" asked Hattie.

"Never. You two are going with me."

"Not me." Linda removed her glasses and shot Emily a matter-of-fact look. "I have two books to read before I head home Sunday. You and Hattie go. I'll enjoy being out on the lanai alone." She shoved her glasses back on and opened her book.

Emily turned to Hattie. "Is that okay with you? Maybe I can see if Charlie's friend Ted can join us."

"His friend? It's about time some romance headed my way."

Emily laughed and put her hand on Hattie's arm. "Don't get your hopes up, girl. He seems to be rather reserved."

"You know what they say, opposites attract." Hattie fluffed her curls.

"You sure this is okay with you, Linda?" asked Emily.

Linda lowered the book to her lap. "I know this is hard for you two to believe, but I actually enjoy having my alone time. How soon do you think you can be out of the house?"

"Okay, that's my answer." Emily wondered how long it would be before the reality of what had transpired would hit her. A lasting relationship had suddenly become a possibility, but she wouldn't call Jen again just yet. "Linda, give me your honest opinion. You have a business head about you. What are the probabilities I could have all of Cameron Consultants turned over into someone else's hands by the end of March next year?"

Linda slapped the book closed. "What? You're not thinking of staying here, are you?"

"Here I thought you two were all for it."

Hattie swung her feet into the aisle. "Girl, did the man ask you to marry him?"

A dreamy smile crossed Emily's face. "I believe he will

before my feet leave the Florida sand."

"I don't think the board will go for that," said Linda.

"It's not the board's choice. Stan had it written into the agreement. I could quit tomorrow if I wanted to. Carson would take over. However, I'm not about to send the business to an early grave and all the employees with it."

Hattie's voice croaked with approval. "Honey, you've had a hardworking life and I, for one, think you should feel free to do whatever you want to do. Can I be your maid of honor?"

Linda stuffed her book into her purse. "How are you going to approach the board?"

"Everything hinges on what Charlie does in the next few days. If he does what I think he will do, I'll put off telling the board for another week. I'll already be staying down here a few more days to make sure my business anchor's going to take hold." Emily's cell rang. "Hi, Charlie. Do you miss me already?"

"Of course, I do, Mrs. Cameron."

She squirmed in her seat. "You're being so formal."

"It's called being polite."

"Too polite."

"I don't think I'll be able to make it tonight."

Emily's stomach dropped. "Was it something I said?"

"It didn't take me long to realize I'm not going to bounce back to normal in a few hours' time. I'll be okay by tomorrow."

Emily stuck what was left of her thumbnail in her mouth. "I told the girls as much. Shall I come there?"

"I would like to say yes, but I'm afraid I'm going to have to call it a day, already. Would tomorrow work?"

Emily muffled her sigh as she sprang back into corporate mode. "I understand completely. If there's anything at all I can get you or do for you, please don't hesitate to call me."

"I do want to plan something for tomorrow. Can I call you in the morning?"

"I'm up by six, Charlie."

"Walking, I suppose."

She smiled. "Yes, that's my regimen. And I'd be glad to walk with you, too, sometime tomorrow."

"I'll call you around nine, and we'll make plans."

Emily nuzzled the phone and closed her eyes. "I'll wait to hear from you."

"Emily?"

"Yes?"

"I love you."

sixteen

"Nice sweat suit. How long have you had that stuck in the back of your closet?" Ted grinned.

"It's a little wrinkled, but it will do. It's only going to get sweaty anyway. I thought we'd go about half a mile and back for our first time." Charlie continued down the street.

"I didn't put on my workouts just to go a half mile. I think you can press yourself a little more than that."

Charlie shook his head. "I'm talking about the corner at the stop sign. That's all for now. A certain lady promised to walk with me today, too. I'd much rather be in her company."

"I'm like a cheap Model T. I've been traded just when I've given you the best years of my life. Look, it's time to turn around already."

"Ha." Charlie smacked Ted on the back. "You be good to me, and I'll let you in on a little secret."

"What?"

"You know, she has two friends."

"Unless they're as classy as she is, I'm not interested."

"Aw, come on. It'll be fun."

"It gets too complicated."

"You'd be doing me a huge favor. Emily follows strict principles. If we wanted to dine at my place, she wouldn't do it without someone else there."

They had already made their circle and were back. "I suppose I could this one time. I have two questions. Are the others as nice as she, and are they all leaving on Sunday?"

Lowering himself to the step, Charlie wiped his hand across

his forehead. "Yes to the first, and to the second question, her friends are leaving Sunday, but Emily is staying another week. Trust me, you won't regret it. Now, I'm going to shower and spruce up a bit. You go do the same and meet me back here in an hour. Bring some beach clothes along."

Ted shook his head. "You're a tough man to bargain with. I'll do it, but I'm not sure it's the best idea. These things have a way of turning on a guy."

"If the other two women are anything like Emily, it will be worth your time. Trust me." Charlie fished in his pocket for his cell phone. In ten minutes, it would be nine o'clock. She wouldn't mind if he called early.

❧

Emily massaged another coat of sunscreen over her nose and arms then slipped on her beach robe. Hattie adjusted her sunglasses and pointed toward the gentleman in the distance. "I'd say he's about forty," said Hattie.

Linda sat up straight. "Who is?"

"Right out there in front of me, the one who keeps bending to pick up shells."

"You've got good eyesight," said Linda.

"Why don't you just enjoy the scenery in the distance, Hattie. You won't be here that much longer," said Emily.

"What are you looking at?" Hattie nudged Emily.

"I see hope. I see the person I was meant to be coming back into view. Oh, look. There are the dolphins."

"Where?" Linda sprung to her feet.

Emily stood. "Look off to your left about forty-five degrees from the man Hattie was looking at."

"Ooh, I see." Hattie ran up to the surf then yelled back at them. "There's four of them."

"Where?" said Linda. "Never mind, I see them now. It looks like there's more than four."

With Linda following, Emily walked toward the surf to join Hattie. "See what I mean? There's so much more to look at around here. I love to see stuff like that. It makes me want to stay here forever."

Linda frowned. "I put a pencil to some financial issues the board might present to you. In case you want to see it, I left the paper back at the room. You might want to rethink this plan of yours."

"Yesterday held its own magic. Today may be different. He hasn't called. It's nearly nine thirty. I hope he hasn't changed his mind." Emily nibbled on her thumbnail, suddenly not sure of Charlie's constancy.

"Why would you think he's changed his mind?" asked Hattie.

"You never know."

"Well, do me a favor. Look at the notes I made when you get a chance," said Linda. "Try to keep your emotions intact until you do."

"Linda, I'm not going to spend the rest of my life wondering if I've made all the right decisions. My happiness is important. I don't even feel, right now, like I could go back and run that business. That's Stan's baby, not mine. I only took it because he left me."

"You've built it further than he did." Linda sighed. "Em, he didn't leave you on purpose."

Emily frowned then looked up at Linda. "I know he didn't leave me on purpose. And it's true. I have built the company up. But I didn't have a life while doing it. Now I do." Emily reached her hand into her pocket to get her phone but pulled out her MP3 player instead. "Oh, no. I picked up the wrong thing from the table this morning. How'd I do that?" Emily ran toward the condo with Linda following.

"It's age, my dear. It's age." Linda stood at the bottom of the steps to catch her breath.

"Age is only a state of mind." Emily pushed through the door and scoured the apartment for her phone. "Anyone seen it? I can't find my phone."

Linda opened her phone. "Here, I'll call you."

Strains of "Ode to Joy" began to play. "I hear it!" Emily followed the sound out to the table on the lanai. She flicked her cell open to see she had three messages, all from Charlie. After listening to them, she walked back into the condo. "He wants to meet for lunch. . .all three of us."

Linda waved the girls on. "You two go and enjoy yourselves. Hattie, when you discover two's company and three's a crowd, give me a call on my cell, and we'll meet somewhere."

Hattie shrugged her shoulders. "Okay by me, but I don't mind meeting the gentleman for lunch. You renting a car to get into town?"

"Did you miss it? It's parked between the two palms. I had the same company deliver it. I'll see you all later."

Emily edged the door to her bedroom closed while she dialed Charlie's number.

"Morning, Emily."

"I guess you figured out by now my cell phone got disconnected from me."

"That's a good thing once in a while."

"I'd love to meet for lunch if the invitation is still good."

"We'll pick you up around eleven, is that okay?"

Emily glanced out her window. "We?"

"My friend, Ted, is coming with us. Are Hattie and Linda coming, too?"

"Hattie, yes. Linda has other plans."

"Ted's driving; he's prompt."

"I am, too. Where are we going; how should we dress?"

"It's daytime Florida. We're going to the Waterfront Restaurant, so dress casual. See you soon."

The phone clicked. Emily still held her cell to her ear. Yesterday must have been magical to him, too. Perhaps shyness overtook him today. She had enjoyed hearing the words, *I love you* when they'd ended yesterday's conversation. Perhaps, today, her answer wouldn't stick in her throat.

Emily dressed then peeked in on Hattie. "Just a word, ma'am. Please don't bathe in perfume today. Less is more."

Hattie's face fell. "I'm meeting a new man, and you don't want me to wear perfume?"

"This is Florida. Be fresh. You're amazing without all that extra you pour on."

"I'm getting the hint, if you want to call it that."

Emily threw a crocheted shawl over her arm. "Five minutes, Hattie. If you're ready, let's go down to the bottom of the stairs. I don't want to keep them waiting."

As they approached the bottom, the car pulled up. Emily landed her eyes on Charlie while Hattie's big smile communicated her thoughts. She bumped up against Emily. "You didn't tell me he was so gorgeous."

The men stepped out of the Cadillac at the same time. Ted, a good six inches taller than Charlie, walked toward Emily. While he briefly shook her hand, his eyes shot to Hattie, then back. "Nice to see you again, Mrs. Cameron."

Emily maneuvered Hattie closer to Ted. "This is my friend, Hattie Lincoln, and please, call me Emily."

"Pleased to meet you, Ms. Lincoln. I'm Ted."

Emily shifted her attention to Charlie. He gave a nod to Hattie then turned his gaze on Emily. "You look stunning." He offered his elbow. "Shall we?"

❧

They drove a short distance to the Waterfront Restaurant on the bay. Ted dropped Charlie, Emily, and Hattie at the door to get a place in line while he parked the car. Hattie disappeared into the restroom, leaving Emily alone with Charlie. "Are your grandchildren in sports, Charlie?"

"They both play soccer. I can't make all of their games, but I get to as many as I can. What about yours?"

"One's in basketball, and one's in wrestling in Indy. The two in Portland are in soccer, too. I only get to see them play about once a year."

"I have a feeling they love seeing you when you're there."

"I hope so. I'd love to see them more."

Charlie leaned closer. "I hope you don't mind the long wait. The tourists and locals all like to hop to their favorite place for lunch and get there early. The Waterfront Restaurant takes reservations for dinner, but it's first come, first served at noon." The host of people moved steadily as more tables were seated.

"There's Ted."

"And here comes Hattie the other way. Her smile spreads wider than the state of Texas." He touched the small of her back. "Do you think they'll hit it off as well as we did?"

Emily felt the warmth of his whispers against her cheek. The enchantment still lingered. She feared saying anything would make the moment disappear. She cast him a sideways glance. "I'm glad to hear you feel we've hit it off."

"I thought that was obvious."

The hostess turned to Charlie. "Table for four?"

"Here we go." Charlie took Emily's hand as he followed the hostess to a table in the front corner by the window. An expansive view of the bay spread across the backdrop. He motioned to Ted then helped Emily with her chair. He was seated to her left.

"I wondered where you two lovebirds went," said Hattie.

Charlie shot Emily a look. "I like that term."

Ted laughed. "Hattie, you have amazing insight. Maybe you

and I should go off somewhere by ourselves and leave them alone."

"You people are impossible." While Emily acted embarrassed, secretly, she enjoyed thinking of herself belonging in a relationship with Charlie.

Ted opened his menu as the waiter arrived at their table. "Hey, let's eat then go to some of those shops down the block. I bet the girls would like that. May I order for you, Hattie?"

"I'll have the BLT on toast and a water, please."

"What would you like, Emily?" asked Charlie.

"I'll have that chicken sandwich on the multigrain bun with water to drink, thanks."

"The young lady will have the grilled chicken sandwich, and I'll have the grouper sandwich." He turned to Emily. "Do you want slaw with that?"

"Please."

He turned back to the waiter. "We'll have the slaw, and we'll both have water with lemon. Ted?"

"You can bring me the waterfront burger with lettuce and tomato only, thanks, and water."

Hattie inched closer to Ted. "I love shopping. We went for a little bit, yesterday, but I'm already beginning to go into shock without somewhere else to spend some more money. It's better shopping out here than going in town to the mall."

Ted caught Hattie's attention. "So, you've seen some of the stores already?"

"Not nearly enough."

"She wanted to head south to Sarasota yesterday, but we ran out of time," said Emily.

Ted still focused on Hattie. "I'd be glad to take you down there, Hattie. That's one place I do like to shop."

Ted continued to expound to Hattie about each store he had shopped at on St. Armand's Key and how much she could expect to spend on a day's shopping spree. Meanwhile, a former acquaintance of Charlie's strolled by the table and struck up a conversation with him and Emily.

After about twenty minutes, the waiter brought the food to the table. Emily felt Charlie's warm hand enclose hers. Ted took Hattie's hand as she reached for Emily's. When Charlie finished his prayer of thanks, Hattie's exuberant closing travelled to the next table where a young man and his family echoed her "amen."

Charlie gave Emily's hand a squeeze then spread his napkin on his lap.

"What kind of business are you in, Hattie?" asked Ted.

"I'm in office interior design. I went to school for fashion design, but that's a hard business to break into."

"Where can we get her in around here, Charlie? Would Rog be interested?"

Charlie shook his head as he swallowed his food. "Why don't you get her an appointment with the guy that took over your office building? Roger just redecorated after I left."

Ted laughed. "At least she could deduct her trip down here then."

Emily blotted her lips with a napkin. "I do have to say, your son's office is beautifully decorated with revealing family photos."

Charlie took a gulp of water then cupped his hand over Emily's. "At least now you know who I am."

"This sandwich is delicious." She knew changing the subject didn't fool anyone, but she didn't mind. She was having fun with the man sitting next to her. However, time was of the essence. While she had already made her mind up about Charlie, could he come to a decision, just as quickly, about her?

❧

Lunch drifted into an afternoon walk. The afternoon walk

lingered into dinner. After dinner, Ted and Hattie went to a movie in town while Charlie and Emily went for a drive. Charlie drove across the bridge to Perico Island and pulled the car off into the sand, facing the water. "I love to sit here and watch the scenery."

Emily wrapped her shawl around her shoulders. "The view is amazing."

"It's peaceful. Every so often, there's a shooting star, if you happen to be looking in the right direction."

"Have you ever been out on the water at night in your boat?"

"It's more than spectacular. I wish we could go out sometime together."

"I do, too, as long as I don't get seasick again."

Charlie took her hand. "I'd drive slowly and stay away from big waves."

She laughed. "Somehow, I believe you. Perhaps we can go since I'm staying until next Sunday."

"Do your children know you're staying longer?"

"I called Jennifer and let her know. My grandchildren wanted to ditch school and join me down here. For a moment, I thought she was going to let them."

"How old are they?"

"Jennifer's are fifteen and sixteen."

"Will they all want to be with us when we really get old?"

"Do you worry about it?"

Charlie shuffled in his seat. "Somewhat. My trip to the hospital made me realize how vulnerable I am. If it weren't for you. . ." Charlie couldn't finish. How could he tell Emily she had made all the difference in his life?

"Charlie, I've learned a valuable lesson. I've tried to do life by just thinking about God now and then. This week, He's shown me that everything I'm looking for can be found in Him. Even if no one would want you and me, He does, and

He accepts us for who we are—young or old, rich or poor."

He squeezed her hand as he caught a glint in her eye. He found himself wishing he had even more time than another week. This beautiful woman was about to be snatched from him and sent back to Indiana. "Emily, can we have breakfast together tomorrow? I have so much to say, but something is preventing me from saying it."

"I would love to meet for breakfast. You tell me where, and I'll be there."

Charlie's heart melted at her eagerness. "I'll have breakfast all ready at my place. My cleaning girl, Tess, wants to handle it all." He stared at her for a moment and contemplated taking her in his arms, but he knew he wouldn't want to let her go. "With that, I think we better go."

She raised her brows. "Whatever you say."

The wheels were turning in his head as he drove back out to the beach. He'd serve her breakfast and spring the question. Right now, he couldn't think about it. "This is a nice time to travel. No tourists."

Emily leaned closer to him. "Like me?"

"You're excluded. You traveled out here in my shuttle." He leaned in her direction as he turned into her drive.

"Thank you, Charlie. I can't remember when I've enjoyed a day so much." Emily reached for the door handle.

"Wait. Let me get that for you." He clicked the release on his seat belt and walked around the car to open her door. He reached for her hand.

Emily started walking. "I can find my way from here."

"I would prefer to walk with you."

"You would? I'd like that."

He took her elbow as they walked up the stairs. Emily's pointed politeness had him worried he hadn't moved fast enough. "I sense that you've learned to fend for yourself."

She pulled her elbow away and looped her arm through his. "You're right. After that speech to you about God, I need to learn to lean. Can you help me?"

As they reached the top of the stairs, he started to answer, but the door opened. "Well, it took y'all long enough to get back here. Ted brought me home an hour ago."

"Did you have fun, Hattie?" Emily sounded disappointed to see her.

Charlie rested his arm over Emily's shoulder. "If you ladies will excuse me, I'll be taking off now. Emily, do we have a date for breakfast?"

"I'll be there. What time?"

"Eight o'clock, okay?"

"That's fine, Charlie. I'll see you then."

seventeen

Tess dried the last palm-tree-patterned plate and set it on the counter with the others. "Why didn't you just use the dishwasher?"

Charlie stacked the dinner plates and sandwich plates together to carry out to the deck. "Because Nancy always took special care with these dishes. She tried to teach me that the fast way was not always the best way. Can you open the door for me?"

"Wait, let me spread the tablecloth first." Tess took the damask cloth outside and flapped it twice in the air before she floated it over the table. Then she opened the door for Charlie. "There you go. I'll get the glasses."

He positioned each of the place settings so that he and Emily could sit next to each other. Tess walked out with two crystal tumblers and handed them to him. "Thanks, Tess. What would I do without you here to help me?" Charlie placed the glasses upside down until just before Emily came. "Where are the flowers, Tess?"

"I'll get them out of the fridge." She retrieved five red roses wrapped in cellophane and brought them outside. "Here you go."

Charlie settled three of the roses in a vase set in the center of the table and one each at her place setting and his. "How's that look?"

"Almost better than my food." She walked back in the house and he followed.

He tasted some of the fresh peaches and grapes that lay

assembled in a bowl that sat inside another bowl filled with ice. Then he lifted the lid from the skillet that hid the turkey bacon and eggs, which made up the main course.

Tess directed his attention to the opened refrigerator door. "Okay, inside here, you'll find plain low-fat yogurt surrounded by a bed of fresh strawberries and blueberries. Also, I've arranged sliced tomatoes, oranges, and apples on a bed of lettuce leaves. Don't touch any of it until Emily gets here."

"Aw, Tess. You're no fun." Charlie eyed the clock above the sink. Emily would be here in less than an hour. "You're a better chef than I thought."

"You don't know the half of it, Mr. Parish. My mama was always busy working, so I was put in charge of the cooking. I came up with all sorts of things without having to spend a lot of money."

"I don't want to change the subject from breakfast, but do you do a lot of vegetable cooking?"

"Of course. I go pretty much meatless."

"One of these days you're going to show me how to make these vegetables taste good. All I know how to do is steam them."

Tess tapped his fingers. "I'd be glad to help you when I can. Maybe you should hire me part-time to be your cook. Hector would like that. He wouldn't have to run me all over town to cleaning jobs."

Charlie leaned up against the kitchen counter. "I'm going to think that over. That might be the best idea you've ever come up with."

Tess wiped her hands on her apron. "Are you serious about your lady friend?"

He nodded. "I think I am."

"At your age you're blessed to find someone."

"At my age? You're teasing me, aren't you?" He winked at

her. "It's easy to find women down here. I've found more than just a woman. I've found a friend, too."

She pointed to the door. "Is that her who just drove in?"

Charlie parted the blinds on the kitchen window. "Oh no. It's Roger. It's not time to let him in on things yet. What am I going to do?"

"Do you want me to tell him you're not home?"

"I'll just have to face him."

Tess walked over to the window. "Well, you better get ready, he ran up two steps at a time, and he's standing out there with his hands on his hips, looking at your table."

"God help me, here I go." Charlie opened the door and stepped out onto the deck.

"You expecting company, Dad? That's a nice table, nice table."

"I am expecting someone. In fact, there she is now." Charlie motioned to Emily who was walking up the block from the trolley stop.

Roger's mouth dropped open as he spied Emily then swiveled back to Charlie. "Mrs. Cameron?"

"Careful now, son, don't want you falling off the deck." Charlie chuckled and patted Roger on the back. Then he turned his attention to the eye-catching woman walking toward his steps.

Charlie walked halfway down to meet her. "Good morning, Emily. You're just in time to see Roger." He whispered, "I think he's surprised to see you."

"Good morning, Mr. Parish." Emily stretched her hand out to Roger as she topped the steps. "Are you joining us for breakfast?"

"Well. . ."

Charlie patted Roger on the back. "Good idea, will you join us?"

Roger adjusted his attention to Emily. "I don't suppose you're here on business, Mrs. Cameron, are you?"

"Roger, Emily is here because I invited her to relax and have breakfast with me."

"So are you saying this is a date?"

Emily broke in. "Mr. Parish, why don't you sit with us? I would love to get to know you better."

Roger acknowledged her invitation. Charlie went into the house to inform Tess that his son would be staying for breakfast also. Tess whirled in anger and started speaking in Spanish. "Calm down, honey. He didn't know that I had this morning planned."

When he walked back out on the deck, Emily and Roger were involved in a lively discussion about the citrus business. Tess followed him out with an extra setting of everyday white stoneware. "Here, Mr. Parish. You can sit here. That seat is for your father, God bless him."

Tess then brought out the silver fruit bowl and set it in the middle of the table. When she returned the next time, she brought cream and sugar in silver servers. Charlie waited for her to go back inside then took the opportunity to talk to Roger.

He rested his hand on Roger's forearm and noticed a smile on Emily's face. "Rog, I have something important to tell you." Charlie put his other hand over Emily's as it rested at the edge of her plate. "I invited Mrs. Cameron here today with the intention," he paused, then blurted the rest out, "with the intention of asking for her hand in marriage."

Emily's hand turned to jelly as her fork dropped and landed straight up in the center of a strawberry. Her eyes teared as she stared at Charlie.

"Now, I know this is shocking to both of you and not too romantic for you, Emily, but I don't have too much courage when it comes to something like this, so when I was ready, I had to say it."

Roger's mouth hung open, as he seemed to look for confirmation from Emily.

Emily's voice came in whispers. "Oh, my dear, sweet Charlie. . .I accept."

Charlie stood from the table and walked around to Emily. He took her hands in his. "I love you, Emily."

I'm a flash, she stood and threw her arms around his neck. "Soon-to-be Mrs. Parish. I love you, too, Charlie."

Roger cleared his throat. "Excuse me, I don't want to be in the way. I'll see myself to the car."

Charlie released his embrace. "Rog, you'll come to the wedding, won't you?"

"I—I imagine we'll come. When will it be? Next year this time?"

"Our wedding, if Emily agrees, will take place sooner than that."

Roger nodded to Emily. "Congratulations. Forgive my surprise." He stopped at the top of the steps. "How soon, Dad?"

"I was thinking by the end of next week would work out."

Roger's tone cooled. "Why so soon, Dad? Why don't you give it some time? I know Mrs. Cameron is extremely likeable, but you two don't really know each other—no offense, Mrs. Cameron."

"Stop and think about it, Rog. I'm not at the age where I can afford to think about it." Charlie winked at Emily.

"Will you do prenups?"

Charlie's mouth dropped open as he glanced at Emily.

"Good idea," said Emily. "That would be beneficial for both our families, Charlie. I don't mind doing that at all."

Roger's shoulders relaxed. "Thank you, Mrs. Cameron. Thank you."

Once again, Charlie was amazed at Emily's charm and grace. While many women would have reacted differently, she calmed Roger instantly to the point where he even seemed to accept the marriage proposal.

"Joyce and I will come. Give me a day's notice, Dad. Give me a day's notice." Roger reached out his hand to shake Charlie's, but Charlie embraced him instead. As he passed Emily, he shook her hand and congratulated her. "I ⌐ this means you and I will have more than a business rel ⌐ ship, Mrs. Cameron. I gotta get home and tell Joyce. She'll more surprised than I was."

As Roger took three steps at a time, Charlie gave Emily a slow, deliberate wink. He clasped his fingers through hers as they watched Roger pull out of the drive. When he was out of sight, Charlie turned and pulled Emily into his arms. He rubbed his cheek against hers and lightly brushed it with his lips. When he released his embrace, Charlie smiled. "I guess we better start making plans."

❧

"Okay, let's work down this checklist. Did you get the license?" Linda followed Emily through the special occasion section of women's wear in Nordstrom's in Tampa.

"Of course. That was the first thing we did on Friday." Emily lifted a dress from the rack. "How about this one?"

"Nope, bad for your coloring. Did you get the minister who's going to marry you?"

Emily held the dress in front of herself and looked in the mirror. "Yes. I went to church with Charlie on Sunday, and we talked to his pastor. Everything's set." She hung the dress back.

"Got a place for all the kids to stay?"

"You know I've already done that. They're staying in the same complex where I got all of us another condo. His kids are staying at his home for the weekend."

"Then where are you staying after you're married?"

"We're taking a very short honeymoon to the Bahamas."

"And then. . . ?"

"He offered to accompany me back to Indiana until I have all the business ends tied up. I personally contacted Carson. Thanks for not letting him in on anything until I spoke with him."

"How 'bout this one, Emily?" Hattie glided in front of Linda to look in the mirror. The floral burnout gown she wore was more than brief in places that should have been covered.

Linda pushed Hattie back into the dressing room. "Hattie, this is Emily's wedding you flew back here for. You're hanging all out of that dress. Not appropriate."

"It's hot on the beach this week."

"Not that hot."

"What are you wearing? I hope you're going to take it to the next level and dress formally. Oh, whose phone is that?"

"It's not mine." Linda glanced at Emily.

Emily focused her eyes on the rack in front of her. *This is it.* She lifted a beaded chiffon gown from the rack and held it up. "I'm trying this on. Will someone try to find my phone in my purse and see who it is?"

Hattie plunged her hand inside the handbag and came up with the phone, which had already quit ringing. "It's Jennifer's number on the display. Should I call her back?"

Emily nodded as she backed slowly toward the dressing room.

The phone rang again. "Emily's phone, Hattie here."

Hattie raised her brows to Emily and mouthed the words, "Are you here?"

"Tell her I'll call her back in about thirty minutes."

"Jen, how are you, honey? She's trying on some dresses, shall I have her call you?"

As Hattie pulled in her stomach and stared at herself in the mirror, she nodded to Emily. "Jennifer, your mom has already run this past you, right?"

Emily walked toward Hattie as she gently reinforced Emily's decision to marry Charlie.

"If I were you, I wouldn't worry a bit. Your mom is a smart, classy woman. She knows how to size up a man. Believe me, she has found a gem." Hattie lifted her shoulders and tugged at the bodice of the dress she had tried on. "As soon as you see them together, you'll understand. They just fit together. Now, get those kids out of school, grab the hubby, and get down here, hon. She wants you here."

Hattie stood nodding her head for a few seconds. "Got it, honey. See you then." She flipped the phone shut and gave Emily a thumbs-up. "The kids and Jennifer are coming. Jason is trying to get on the same flight as them and will fly in Friday to Sarasota. They'll head to the condo you told her you had rented. They're going to rent a car in Sarasota and be out to the beach around nine o'clock in the evening."

Emily let out a nervous breath. "Thanks, Hattie, for smoothing things over. Now, I need to try on my wedding dress." She disappeared into one of the dressing rooms.

After about ten minutes, Emily appeared in her stunning gown. "Well, girls. What do you think?" She twirled in front of them then stood facing the center of the three-way mirror. Her fingers ran along the beaded pattern on the bodice then down to rustle against the chiffon.

"I love that blue," said Hattie. "Are you sure you don't want to wear white?"

"It's teal, and Charlie loves this color. I think this will show up beautifully against the waters of the Gulf."

From behind, Linda rested her hands on Emily's shoulders and leaned against her. "You make the dress beautiful. I had a feeling something like this was going to happen down here. Didn't I mention when we had our phone conversation the day before we left one of us needed to get lucky?"

Emily turned around. "Yes, you did mention that, but I want you to know it had nothing to do with luck. God saw two successful but lonely people who weren't ready to spend the rest of their lives alone."

"I have to say it, Emily. You've seem to have returned to the Emily I knew in college. In spite of all your difficulties, you trusted fully in God for everything, back then. I believe you drifted away from that for a time."

"You noticed?"

"I noticed."

"I guess that just goes to show, you don't know who's watching your life. I hope you see that only the Lord could have brought us together the way He did." She walked back to the mirror and studied the dress.

"And Charlie believes that, too," said Linda.

Emily nodded. "That's the amazing part."

Linda pulled a pad of paper from her purse. "I hate to bring this up, but what about the board?"

"Linda, whatever the board members want to think, they're going to think. I'm trusting you to keep this whole thing under wraps until I get back to set everyone straight on what happened."

"Oh Em, do you like this gown I'm wearing?" asked Hattie.

Emily scanned the dress in seconds. "I love the colors and the scarf detail. It's just not me."

"Is it me?"

"That's a loaded question, Hattie. Why don't we leave it this way? If you can have them do something to raise the fabric level closer to the neckline, it will be more appropriate."

"Oh, you guys. You're going to have me wearing clothing with turtlenecks one of these days. By the way, Em, I saw some gorgeous satin shoes over at the shoe counter. They'd look great with that dress you have on."

Emily shook her head. "We'll be on the beach, hon. I'm wearing flip-flops."

"Oh Emily, no," said Linda.

"Charlie and I both will be wearing them with our dress clothes. I don't want to ruin an eighty-dollar pair of shoes in sinking sand."

"How dreadful to think of me wearing flip-flops. I'm at least wearing my two-inch heels." Hattie disappeared for a few minutes and returned with jewelry in her hands. "Look, hon. Here's some toe rings you can wear. They're only twenty dollars each. They say *faith*, *hope*, and *love*. Aren't they cute? And look at these crystal chandelier earrings. If you're wearing flip-flops on the bottom, at least wear fancy jewelry on the top."

Laughing, Emily gave in. "Okay, I'll wear the earrings, not the toe rings. You wear the toe rings." She twirled again in front of the mirror. "This is it, girls. This is the dress I'm going to wear on my wedding day. Let me go change and see how soon they can have this all pressed and ready to go. I need to get out of here. My future husband and I are meeting to watch the sunset tonight!"

Emily changed back into her beige walking shorts and cranberry shell, then arranged the lined gown on the hanger. In a matter of days, she would marry the man she loved on the beach in front of his house.

eighteen

The tie hung crooked. Charlie yanked it from his neck and started over. "Help me get this tie fixed, Dan."

"Dad, it looked great. I could never tie it any better."

Charlie stood in front of the mirrored closet doors as he wrapped one end of the tie around the other, twice. Then he yanked the tie from his neck. "I should've worn my blue Hawaiian shirt, then I wouldn't have to mess with this thing."

Dan stepped in front of him and took the tie from his hand. "You look dashing in your tux. Let me help you with that tie. Wasn't Mom the one who always had to fix it for you?"

Charlie watched Dan's face as he worked with the tie. "I'm glad you flew in for the wedding, and I'm thrilled to hear your screenplay has been accepted."

After Dan finished, he stood next to Charlie and looked in thπe mirror. "There you go, Dad. You look amazing."

Charlie threw his arms around his youngest son.

"I wouldn't have missed the wedding. I'm thrilled you've found someone else to complete your life, Dad. Even Roger likes Emily. At least he and Joyce will quit hounding you to move into the city, now."

Charlie smoothed the front of his tux. "He meant well, Dan. Roger and Joyce only want the best for me. By the way, hand me my flip-flops over there on the chair."

"Dad, you're pretty cool. Are you really going to wear these?" Dan smacked his dad on the back.

"Of course, Emily is, too. We're going to be standing in the sand. What else do you wear in the sand?"

"Do you have another pair? I think we still wear the same size."

Charlie motioned to the closet. "Slide open the door. There's at least four pairs in there."

"Cool, Dad. I'm wearing them, too."

The grin on Dan's face hadn't changed since he was a kid. The joy of seeing him happy was worth a million to Charlie. He hoped Emily's kids would show the same delight. "What time is it?"

Dan pointed to the clock on the bureau. "You have less than an hour to go, Dad. Are you excited?"

He nodded his head. "More than I've been in a long time."

"Were you this excited the first time?"

"I was."

Dan sank onto the bed. "You really loved Mom, didn't you?"

Charlie sat next to him. "With all my heart."

"I'm really glad you're marrying again. That's the type of man you are. I hope I can be as successful in love someday as you are."

"You're nearly forty, Dan. When can I expect a new daughter-in-law?"

"Well, actually, I've met someone at the church I go to in LA. This could finally be it."

Charlie embraced his son again. "I can't believe it. I've been waiting a long time for that news."

"After Penny died, I didn't think I could love again. Rachel is proving me wrong."

"Keep me informed." Charlie glanced out the window. "Oh my. The guests are arriving. Look out there on the beach."

"When do you go down?"

Charlie stood, then felt for his wallet in his pocket. "I probably better go right now. I'm not to see the bride arrive out front."

"I'm with you, Dad. Let's go."

☙

The day couldn't have been more perfect. Ted arrived to pick the girls up. Jennifer, her children, and Jason, who had gotten in around ten the night before, met Ted at the condo, then followed him and the girls to Charlie's house. Emily spent the twenty minutes to the wedding site dabbing tears from her professionally made-up eyes. "Thanks for picking us up, Ted. I don't think I could have gotten here on my own."

"This is an important day for me. I get to drive the bride to her groom and get the bonus of transporting two other beautiful ladies at the same time." He adjusted his mirror to face more toward Hattie.

Emily caught the wink from Hattie to Ted. Linda dabbed almost as many tears as Emily. She turned to see if Jen and Jason still followed behind. Jared's wife and kids couldn't get away, but Jared promised to be there in time for the wedding and planned to meet everyone at Charlie's. Emily's heart soared at the vote of confidence from two of her children the night before. God was working all things out for a smooth wedding today.

A hand stuffed full of tissues emerged from the backseat. Emily turned her face and nodded her thanks to Linda, then swiveled toward Ted. "Do you have your saxophone?"

"Yes, ma'am. It's snug in the trunk."

"Is this really happening to me?" Charlie's closeness from the night before still protected her. The sunset's purples, pinks, and lilacs had never been more impressive. They refused to part for more than an hour after the sun disappeared. In spite of possible problems with blending, which seemed to have calmed, they made enduring promises.

"We're here, ladies. Let me go out to the beach and get set up." Ted pushed the button to pop the trunk then twisted to smile at Hattie before getting out of the car.

"Do I see love blooming for someone else in this Cadillac?" asked Linda.

"Not so fast," said Hattie. "I like Ted, but we don't have the Emily and Charlie gene."

"That's so sad," said Emily.

"Not for me, honey. Ted's one handsome hunk of man, but neither he nor I want to hook up quite that quickly. We're going to keep in touch, though. He's flying up to Indy on the fourth."

Emily twisted partway around. "No kidding?"

Hattie leaned over the front seat. "Enough of us. Are you going to be okay down here all by your lonesome with no one but that man waiting out there for you?"

Emily nodded. "I feel like I've waited for him forever."

Hattie ran her hand along Emily's cheek. "I'm so happy for you, honey. I'm gonna miss you like the dickens, and I think that man you're waiting for is ready. I see Ted waving us to come down to the beach."

"This is it!" Linda fumbled nervously with the back door and raced around to open Emily's door.

Jared rushed toward her with open arms. "Mom, you're beautiful."

"Jared, I had begun to wonder if you were coming or not."

"I had some reservations, at first, but you have a good head on your shoulders. I think I can trust your judgment."

Emily glanced behind her. "Could the kids come?"

"Soccer tournament. They send their love, though, and put in their request for tons of photos." Jared held her for a while then joined Jennifer out on the beach.

Jason walked toward her and held his hand out to her. "I get to escort you to your husband-to-be, Mom. Linda, are you and Hattie both Mom's attendants?"

"No, Jason, I want to watch." Linda wrapped her arms around Jason before she headed out to join the other guests.

Savoring every moment, Emily looped her arm into Jason's. Hattie wobbled on her heels as she preceded Emily to the altar. Jason started moving as soon as Hattie kicked off her shoes and gave a glance back toward them. Ted began to play

"At Last" on his sax.

Random tourists and locals gathered on the beach, close to the water, to witness the ceremony. About thirty friends and family stood around an altar of brass, which was anchored in the sand near the house. Charlie's face shone with excitement. Emily drew in a quick breath when her eye caught him standing there with Dan and Roger by his side.

Jason escorted her slowly, his hand covering his mother's, which wrapped around his arm. "You're beautiful, Mom. I'm so glad Dad married you."

As she floated to the brass altar, Emily smiled her greetings to each friend and family member who had assembled. "I wouldn't have you if I hadn't married Dad, honey."

"You wouldn't have Jared, either. He's a great brother."

She focused in on Charlie. "And what about Jen?"

"She's almost like another mother to me, and she has some weird ideas sometimes, Mom, but I love her."

"Me, too." Emily squeezed his arm a little tighter.

"She'll love having another father. She's the type of woman who needs that affirmation."

"Now, when did you go and get all this wisdom?"

"Here we are." Jason stopped in front of the pastor and Charlie, then hugged Emily. He placed her hand in Charlie's, then moved behind her.

After their vows, Charlie took the simple gold band from Roger's hand and placed it on Emily's finger. She took the matching ring from Hattie and placed it on Charlie's finger.

While they waited together to be pronounced husband and wife, Charlie whispered in her ear. "I've loved you since last Friday, Emily Parish."

She turned and searched his eyes. "And I have loved you for just as long."

A Letter To Our Readers

Dear Reader:
In order that we might better contribute to your reading enjoyment, we would appreciate your taking a few minutes to respond to the following questions. We welcome your comments and read each form and letter we receive. When completed, please return to the following:

Fiction Editor
Heartsong Presents
PO Box 719
Uhrichsville, Ohio 44683

1. Did you enjoy reading *Tropical Island Vows* by Donna L. Rich?
   ❑ Very much! I would like to see more books by this author!
   ❑ Moderately. I would have enjoyed it more if

   _____

   _____

   _____

2. Are you a member of **Heartsong Presents**? ❑ Yes ❑ No
   If no, where did you purchase this book? _____

   _____

3. How would you rate, on a scale from 1 (poor) to 5 (superior), the cover design? _____

4. On a scale from 1 (poor) to 10 (superior), please rate the following elements.

   ____ Heroine   ____ Plot
   ____ Hero   ____ Inspirational theme
   ____ Setting   ____ Secondary characters

5. These characters were special because? _____

_____

_____

6. How has this book inspired your life? _____

_____

_____

7. What settings would you like to see covered in future
   Heartsong Presents books? _____

_____

_____

8. What are some inspirational themes you would like to see
   treated in future books? _____

_____

_____

9. Would you be interested in reading other **Heartsong
   Presents** titles?   ❑ Yes   ❑ No

10. Please check your age range:
   ❑ Under 18   ❑ 18-24
   ❑ 25-34   ❑ 35-45
   ❑ 46-55   ❑ Over 55

Name _____

Occupation _____

Address _____

City, State, Zip _____

E-mail _____

ILLINOIS
WEDDINGS

The past collides with the future in these three riveting romances set in Galena, Illinois. Can Angel, Jeanie, and Ruby survive the impact?

Contemporary, paperback, 368 pages, 5.1875" x 8"

Please send me _____ copies of *Illinois Weddings*. I am enclosing $7.99 for each. (Please add $4.00 to cover postage and handling per order. OH add 7% tax. If outside the U.S. please call 740-922-7280 for shipping charges.)

Name _____

Address _____

City, State, Zip _____

To place a credit card order, call 1-740-922-7280.
Send to: Heartsong Presents Readers' Service, PO Box 721, Uhrichsville, OH 44683

HEARTSONG
PRESENTS

If you love Christian romance…

$12.⁹⁹

You'll love Heartsong Presents' inspiring and faith-filled romances by today's very best Christian authors…Wanda E. Brunstetter, Mary Connealy, Susan Page Davis, Cathy Marie Hake, and Joyce Livingston, to mention a few!

When you join Heartsong Presents, you'll enjoy four brand-new, mass-market, 176-page books—two contemporary and two historical—that will build you up in your faith when you discover God's role in every relationship you read about!

Mass Market 176 Pages

Imagine…four new romances every four weeks—with men and women like you who long to meet the one God has chosen as the love of their lives…all for the low price of $12.99 postpaid.

To join, simply visit www.heartsong presents.com or complete the coupon below and mail it to the address provided.

✂ -

YES! Sign me up for Heartso♥ng!

NEW MEMBERSHIPS WILL BE SHIPPED IMMEDIATELY!
Send no money now. We'll bill you only $12.99 postpaid with your first shipment of four books. Or for faster action, call 1-740-922-7280.

NAME _____

ADDRESS _____

CITY _____ STATE _____ ZIP _____

MAIL TO: HEARTSONG PRESENTS, P.O. Box 721, Uhrichsville, Ohio 44683
or sign up at WWW.HEARTSONGPRESENTS.COM